CU00868592

The journey of seagulls

by

Agnieszka Dryjas-Makhloufi

Published by New Generation Publishing in 2021

Copyright © Agnieszka Dryjas-Makhloufi 2021

First Edition

The author asserts the moral right under the Copyright, Designs and Patents Act 1988 to be identified as the author of this work.

All Rights reserved. No part of this publication may be reproduced, stored in a retrieval system or transmitted, in any form or by any means without the prior consent of the author, nor be otherwise circulated in any form of binding or cover other than that which it is published and without a similar condition being imposed on the subsequent purchaser.

ISBN

| | Paperback | 978-1-80031-658-4 |
| | Ebook | 978-1-80031-657-7 |

www.newgeneration-publishing.com

New Generation Publishing

The **Book**Challenge

WHAT'S YOUR STORY?

This book was shortlisted in the Pen to Print
Book Challenge Competition and has been
produced by
The London Borough of Barking and Dagenham
Library Service - Pen to Print Creative Writing
Programme. This is supported with National
Portfolio Organisation funding from Arts Council,
England.

WHAT'S YOUR STORY?

Connect with Pen to Print
Email: pentoprint@lbbd.gov.uk
Web: pentoprint.org

Supported using public funding by
**ARTS COUNCIL
ENGLAND**

**Barking &
Dagenham**

For my husband, parents and sister

PROLOGUE

I yawned and trotted upstairs to the bedroom. Philip was sound asleep. I watched his face, lit by the moon shining from the open window. His expression was peaceful, his lips slightly parted. I tried to imagine them speaking to me kindly. Tears ran down my cheeks. I plunged beneath the thick duvet, closed my eyes and tried to sleep. A small buzz sounded from a corner of the room. I sat up in bed and switched on the bedside light.

A fly.

Trapped.

I reflected on my past, pictured the sweet face of the girl I used to be, the aroma of boiling home-made noodles my mum prepared for our lunch, the gloomy morning when my dad left us.

At school when they asked me if he died, my cheeks burnt with shame.

'Yes,' I said.

What could I say? That he abandoned our little family?

I checked on Philip again, but his back was turned, and I couldn't see his face. My thoughts returned to the old days once more. I would like to say the good old days, but it was not always easy for a little girl like me at that time. The words and actions of people around me impregnated my soul with pure poison.

I didn't ask why Dad went away. I thought I must have been naughty, or something, that he must have lost patience with me.

Back then, I loved observing the sky, watching the planes soaring up into the wide open space beyond my reach, like birds, their wings carrying them to wherever they wanted. I forgot about the engine deeply hidden within their metal bodies, thinking those planes I watched soar so high possessed that infallible power the birds have.

That is till the day I heard about a plane crash on TV. My mummy told me not to watch the news. She said it was not for the eyes of children. But I wanted to know more about the world. I wanted to travel. I wanted to taste all the yummy food they served in the restaurants and in the movies.

I knew she would laugh at my dreams. I chose to remain silent.

My mum would say of me, 'What a good girl. She is so quiet and never causes any problems.'

Little did she know there was a whole battlefield in the mind of this little girl and a heart full of holes because of the emotions exploding in her every moment of her life like bombs.

She didn't see or feel it. Can I blame her now? Not really. I guess these things were happening to her too – or even worse.

Whenever my mum had an outburst of anger and Dad flung whatever came to hand at her in response, I would tiptoe to my room.

I could make no sense of it. Under the warm duvet my mind and body tried to find peace, and I would cry till I fell asleep. I would awake to find my mum there trying to console me as if only the tears running down my face could draw her attention to my sorrows.

'Hush, Christina, hush,' she'd whisper, 'hush, my darling.'

I'd feel so many emotions in her voice. But she could not soothe me. I knew that beyond the words she spoke, there was no meaning.

Sometimes, I would sit on her lap feeling it was her who needed me to be the parent. I would kiss her forehead, and she kissed mine and we fell asleep in each other's arms.

I always loved roses. My granny grew them in her garden. Her garden was full of life. Busy bees collected pollen and circled above my head. And I would clap and jump with excitement.

The raspberry juice my mum made was the best in the world. I loved looking at my mum's hands. I counted the lines on them and noted all the creased or puffy places hidden in her palm. I imagined them being a big field of adventure. The puffiness was like hills and the lines formed paths. The small red dots were people travelling through fields. And those hands, they worked so hard providing food and so many other things for me.

'Let me play with your hands, Mummy,' I implored when she was busy, though she was always reluctant.

I think she was embarrassed at the condition of her hands.

'Christina, I wish you could stop this silly game of hands. Go play with your dolls or teddies.'

Although I loved my dollies and teddies, I found them boring. I sought something different, something deeper. I wish I could speak to my teddies, but they were always so silent.

Animals were different. A soft purring of a cat made me run after it or talk to it. These were the sacred conversations no one knew about. My imagination ran wild. I imagined being at the theatre. I imagined climbing mountains. I imagined floating in the sky.

When I was a teenager, I was always shy and had a circle of a very few friends whom I could trust. Speaking in front of a large group paralysed me. I was scared they would find me silly or boring.

I studied really hard at school. My dream was to help all the people in the world. In my spare time I would tend to injured birds in parks, and feed stray dogs and cats.

I passed my A-levels with distinction. My teacher was so proud of me.

'You are such a bright girl, Christina. You will go far, you will see,' he said.

I had no idea that kind of praise would motivate me so much. I studied to be a nurse, and passed all my exams with top marks.

My first placement was in an old hospital. I was barely twenty-two years old. I had seen many shocking things in my short life but working on the oncology ward in this place was one of the most harrowing experiences of all – people with cancer waiting for their last treatment, their last chance of life. It was so tough. It was like a nightmare.

This is where I met Philip. He was a doctor on the same ward I worked. Overwhelmed with paperwork and the juggling between patients and their appointments and their relatives, Philip still had time to chat with me.

He was so polite and so handsome, but it was his hands that drew my attention. I was always sort of obsessed with people's hands and the amazing things they could do. Although Philip was a surgeon, his hands were big and appeared very manly to me. I remember thinking they possessed such power. His blonde hair was cut short and he used to frown when he was busy with his work.

I remember that day I spoke to him. I had to see him about a patient. I knocked gently on the door of his office, and went in.

'Doctor Beamers?'

'Yes, Christina?'

He put his paperwork away and looked straight into my eyes.

'I am wondering if we need to change the medicine for one of the patients. He seems very off colour again.'

'I will see him in a minute,' he said, not taking his eyes off me.

I was about to go when he called my name. I stopped.

'Can you please close the door?' he said.

I did as he asked. He was my boss, after all.

'First of all, call me Philip,' he blushed, then corrected himself. 'Doctor Philip.'

I smiled faintly.

'Yes, Phil... Doctor Philip.'

He smiled back to me.

'You work so hard, Christina. You look tired. Why don't you take a day off?'

'I am saving all my days off for vacations,' I said.

'That's reasonable,' he said.

He was blushing. His voice quivered. He tried to say something else, but the words wouldn't come out.

Eventually, he said, 'Christina, will you have dinner with me?'

My eyes widened. My heart told me to be careful. He was my boss. How was I supposed to go for dinner with him?

'I am busy tonight,' I said, trying to avoid looking at him. But he continued to peer straight into my soul.

'How about tomorrow?' he said.

What could I do? I told him tomorrow was fine and returned to my duties.

I sat at home that evening, and I still couldn't believe what had happened. Dr Philip was considered one of the most handsome doctors in our hospital. I was excited, for sure, but I decided not to tell anyone in case any suspicion should be raised about me and Philip.

I looked now at the face of Philip as he slept. Then he changed his position again, tossing and turning as if he was undergoing some sort of stress, even in his dreams.

Then he turned his sleeping face to me again.

There was a puffiness under his eyes that had not been there when we first met.

He married a nurse who of late was questioning what she was doing with her life, dreaming big, like a little girl. Her heart was set on her passion for her art, her soul had discovered her true destiny.

One day I confided in him about my dreams.

'Christina, stop,' he said. 'Use your common sense. You need to keep yourself busy, not think about silly things. Drawing is for children. Artists? They are a bunch of useless people. To be honest, I thought you would advance with your career. You could be a doctor if you wanted. I could help you with that.'

My eyes filled with tears.

'So that's it, isn't it?' I said to him. 'You married Christina, a nurse. Not Christina with all her hopes, dreams and all the stories she wanted to tell?'

'Please, Christina,' he said, 'change the subject.'

That's what Philip always did. Whenever he disliked what I said, he asked me to change the subject.

Always.

As time went by, Philip's outbursts became worse. He accused me of using my nurse's uniform just to attract a doctor like him, and persuaded him to marry. He screamed at me I was only after his money.

It was hard to reason with Philip. He was always right. He always knew what was good for him, and everyone else.

But what if the heart is in a constant search for new experiences? What do we do when what was once good for us does not serve us anymore? I tried to explain this to Philip, but he would not listen.

CHAPTER ONE

Dear Marina,

I am writing to you as I need someone to share my story with. I just can't hold it in anymore. Please forgive me for the burden I am putting on you.

I have just been discharged from a mental hospital. My hospital experience is still holding me back from living my life to the full. My nerves were broken in there. I lost my grip on reality. They told me I was hallucinating and that I had no idea who I was, or who they were. So they increased my medication again and again.

I never had the courage to use my voice.

When I was younger, kids used to laugh at me when they asked if my father ever existed. With tears in my eyes, I would mumble something to them, but deep inside I cried and I shouted: 'How dare you to ask me that, you stupid bastards. Didn't your mother teach you not to ask personal questions?'

Even then, I knew something inside me was broken.

Some of what you are about to read, Marina, you already know. I am writing this all down now so I can make sense of much of it myself. I was the only child in a big family. I felt more owned than loved. I remember asking God – when I was about six – why I existed. Then I asked God if He existed.

As I grew I neither perceived myself as an exceptional beauty nor an ugly person. I was just average. When I entered adulthood, I attracted all sorts of men. What they shared was beautiful features. Beyond that, nothing. No personality, no character. I used to wonder if these men represented a search to replace my father who was absent for the most important events of my young life. I once thought you needed to be a strong character in this life because everything is manipulated, and if you do not stand up and be you, you will not withstand it. But I now know I was wrong. To have a voice means nothing. No one will listen anyway.

Philip was heavily influenced by his parents. They made him think he was weak. And he was. But he learnt that by exerting power over others you can prove your importance. I challenged him many times in the early part of our marriage, and wanted him to discover his strength in a different way.

Relationships are difficult, they say. I don't think they are right. Relationships are extended shadows of ourselves. We fail in seeing that. That's why they seem so difficult.

On many occasions, Philip was a stranger to me. When I told him I had to give up my job, or lose my sanity, he just laughed it off and said: 'Oh, come on, Chris. People have harder lives than yours.' When I tried to explain that I needed a change in life, Philip just shrugged his shoulders. I remember one day, I sobbed my heart out in front of him. He couldn't stand that. He approached me and asked me to stop. When I didn't, Philip walked out and shut the door with such a force that it nearly came off its hinges. I sobbed even louder. Moments later, I heard the front door slam shut as he left the house and didn't come back till the next morning.

This experience shut me down completely from him. I was never able to receive his kisses willingly after that. Silent days came. They were even worse than the arguments. My relatives saw him as a hero saving my life. Little did they know how much I suffered because of his indifference and uncontrolled outbursts of anger. The last scene of that late spring will be forever etched in my heart. After we finally got divorced, he came to me with this pitiful sort of look and said: 'Chris, you know it's all your fault. You ruined it all.' Philip sighed heavily and clenched his fists. I shivered and told him he never had the courage to act like a man, to protect me, to take care of me. I sobbed as he left. This was the end of our marriage and the last time I saw him.

Marina, I miss you very much. I hope to see you very soon.

Love,
Christina

CHAPTER TWO

Once I got on the bus from the airport, I dropped my bag on the bus seat, looked through the window, and let the sun rays caress my cheeks. Oh, how I needed that. I observed the cars and other buses passing by. I saw palm trees dancing in the summer breeze. I looked up into the deep blue sky and saw birds of all kinds circling overhead.

My first contact with Gran Canaria was like that of a baby with its mother: a relationship full of fondness, love, curiosity and constant awe.

I wanted to text Marina, but the view was breath-taking, and I couldn't be bothered to reach my bag. A little pat on my shoulder brought me out of my dream. I turned. An elderly gentleman pointed at the seat next to me and asked politely if he could sit there. I removed my bag and was about to place it on my lap when I realised my other bag – the one with all my money and valuables in, was missing.

The elderly gentleman thanked me and sat down. I tried to remember when I last had my missing bag with me.

Then it came to my mind.

Bus fare.

I paid the driver the bus fare when I entered the bus. I must have had my bag then. It had all important stuff: the wallet with spare change, the other wallet with my savings and debit card, and my phone. Only my ID was with me, in the pocket of my jacket.

Tears burst from my eyes. The gentleman turned to me:

'¿Está bien, señora?'

I nodded.

'Si,' I said, but inside the tears flooded my heart.

I swam in my sorrow. How could I have been so stupid to put my bag on the seat next to me and succumb to the temptation of admiring the views? It was so easy for someone to have just walked past and taken it as I looked out of the window.

Once I got off the bus, I decided to go to the police station and notify them about my loss.

The police officers asked me about the details.

I stood there like a stupid cow.

I mumbled words, but all the Spanish words I knew got stuck in my throat.

'Ha perdiendo… Perdón, he per… perdido mi bo… bolsa.'

The police officer looked straight into my eyes as if trying to guess my nationality.

'¿Señora, de dónde es usted ?'

I stood there not able to answer this question, my hands sweating. I unbuttoned the collar of the sapphire blue shirt I was wearing.

'Do you speak English?' I said.

On the sound of word 'English' I felt the corners of my mouth raise slightly.

The stout police officer with a funny moustache and double chin turned to his younger, more handsome colleague.

'Parece que ella habla inglés. ¿ Puedes hablar con ella?'

The young policeman turned to me and asked me my name, in English.

'Christina Beamers,' I replied.

Beamers. Christina Beamers. My soul ached as the surname left my lips. His surname.

You are a divorced woman, Christina. Philip Beamers belongs to your past.

Tears appeared on my cheeks. I wiped them with my hand.

'I am sorry,' I said. 'I mean Christina B.'

The police officer frowned at me. I bet he thought I was a mad woman.

'What is your surname, madam? Be…? Can you spell it for me?'

He looked at me ready with his pen to note my name down on a form in front of him.

I remembered a book I had once read of a bitterly unhappy woman.

'Bovary,' I said. 'B-o-v-a-r-y.'

The police officer asked me a lot of questions and wrote his report. He promised they would come back to me as soon as they knew anything about my bag.

They asked me to confirm my phone number. My head started spinning when I realised I had left my phone in the bag that had been stolen.

I covered my face with my hands, then I grabbed my other bag, and I ran out of the police station. I ran till I had no more strength in my legs.

I ran till my heart was exhausted.

I ran from Christina Beamers, from Philip Beamers, from all the Beamers I had ever known.

I searched desperately in the pocket of my skirt for the small scrap of paper with my old friend Marina's address on, and a little map she had drawn for me.

I walked along the beach for about fifteen minutes, checking the map again and again. The map led me off the beach to a path in the woods. The smell of pine filled my nostrils. I inhaled the beautiful fragrance, and the few seconds seemed to be eternity. I saw a house that looked like the one my friend had described to me, and gently pushed the gate open.

The house had an old steep roof and reminded me of the ghost stories my friend used to tell me in our university days. Red rose bushes dangled on the fence, just as Marina said, spreading their beautiful fragrance. No other house was nearby. There was silence all around, nothing but the graceful swaying branches of an old tree making music in the wind. The fence around the house stood like its sole protector, a little rickety gate standing guard.

I gently pushed the gate open, and walked though, then knocked at the door with trembling hands.

I checked the door number on the little scrap of paper, and knocked again. After a few seconds I heard someone approaching. A very handsome man opened the door, and stood there gazing at me.

'Can I help you, madam?'

His voice was low and smooth, and his eyes were dark and deep and beautiful.

I blushed, so transfixed by his eyes I could hardly utter a word.

'Madam?' he said.

'I... am... I am... looking for my friend... Marina Hernandez,' I said.

I could feel my cheeks burning red. The stranger's cheekbones so beautifully joined his jawline and his eyes told such a story, I could not take my eyes off his face.

'Marina does not live here anymore,' he said.

I nervously reached into my pocket and showed him the scrap of paper.

'Marina moved to a different place,' he said, kindly, 'but I have no idea where she lives now.'

I thanked the stranger for his time, and he bowed to me so gracefully, and smiled with such sympathy.

The path I followed back to the beach seemed strange, even though it was the same path I had taken to Marina's house. As I walked through a break in the trees, I caught a glimpse of the clear blue sky. The sun pleasantly patted my cheeks, and I felt comforted for a while.

After a few minutes I reached the beach. My arms stretched out and embraced the warmth of the sun. Now I was running with my heart beating wildly and my sandals falling off my feet. The big-bellied sun was going down, wrapping itself in the red blanket of the sky. The sea took the sun in its arms, rocking it like a baby, and the seagulls sang a timeless lullaby.

'Buenas noches,' I murmured as I stopped running to catch the last glimpse of the sun. The dance of colours in the sky took my breath away. It slightly cooled down, so I went to the town centre.

CHAPTER THREE

As the streets emptied the night stepped firmly in, swiftly turning everything into statues. I sat on a bench and gazed up at the starry sky, wishing upon every one of those stars that my luck would change.

'Hola. ¿Como estas?'

I spun my head round quick. An elderly gentleman sat beside me on the bench. How long he had been there, I do not know. Maybe he had always been there.

Too shocked to reply in Spanish, I answered the man in my native tongue.

'I am okay,' I said. 'Thank you.'

The man replied in perfect English.

'Are you not scared?' he said, looking straight into my eyes.

'A little,' I said.

'Where is your home?'

I tried to shrug my shoulders, but it was as if the whole world bore down on them.

'You feel lost,' he said.

The elderly man's tone was strange, as if he knew more about me than I did myself.

I nodded. I had never felt more lost in my life.

'We all feel lost, my dear,' he said, and turned his eyes from me to the stars. I followed his gaze for a moment, searching among the stars for an answer to my woes, then turned to ask him what he meant.

But he was gone.

The morning brought the odour of decaying rubbish from the nearby bins. I stretched on the bench and quickly covered my nose with my hands. Every bone in my body ached and I had never felt so lonely in my entire life.

I spent the day wandering aimlessly through the streets till I could not feel my feet, they were so numb. As the sun began to set, I found myself in a small, empty corner of the market and set up my canvas and began to paint. I had no stool or chair, so sat on my knees. My trembling hands were out of practice as I had not painted for some time, but still I managed to throw some strokes on the canvas.

The shapeless splashes of paint slowly formed into the face of a wizened old man, smiling out from the canvas at me with sparkling eyes and the air of someone older than time itself. I could not see the elderly gentleman properly yesterday, as it was so dark, but I knew this was him.

I carried on painting – without thought as to what I was creating – just letting my brush dance across the canvas, and found myself staring into the eyes of a ginger cat.

My empty stomach rambled. I was so hungry. I searched in the pockets of my skirt in the hope of finding some spare change, but found nothing.

Tears sprang to my eyes but I wiped them away. Painting the old man and the ginger cat had given me an energy, a hope, a need to stand up against the despair I felt. I would not be beaten. I would live by the sale of my paintings. My life would be my art.

By the time the midday sun had climbed high into the sky, I had finished my painting. I leaned the finished canvas against the legs of the easel facing the marketplace so all could view, and attached a small piece of paper with the price of fifteen euros on it. Six hours later, the painting still stood there. No one was interested. My first day living by my art, and it seemed I would go hungry, after all.

At the end of the day, when all the sellers started to pack away their stuff from their stalls, and the busy street life began petering out, I was left alone, with a deepening hole in my soul.

Where I was to go, I did not know. I packed away my canvas, my brushes and the painting, and focussed on finding a warm place to stay for the night.

I was about to be on my way, when I heard behind my back a quiet, rasping voice.

'¡Otra chica de la calle! No tiene nada, solo su propia basura. La pintora de la calle.'

I turned round and replied into the night, my cheeks wet with tears: 'Yes, I *am* a street girl, a painter with nothing but her garbage. Ha ha ha. But one day, you will see, you will see what I will become.'

I took my painting stuff and plodded along the streets looking for a shelter. The cold poured out from the dark corners of the streets, hitting me hard in the face. I went past one house, peeped through the window and spotted a family sitting together by the night lamp. I sighed wistfully. A woman sat comfortably on the sofa and a man, probably her husband, whispered something into her ear which made her smile, and she caressed his face with such affection.

I carried on my way, the cold night breathing into my face, the stars dancing on the blackened canvas they call home. I felt a sudden surge of positive vibrations circulating inside me, filling up my heart and soul, my tiny body now feeling somehow less solitary amidst these houses of total strangers than in the marketplace crowded with people.

I carried on walking, the smell of vanilla floating in the air from a nearby restaurant. The restaurant sat at the end of a blind alley, and I could see a man – perhaps the owner – closing the doors for the night. He held a bulging blue refuse sack in his hands, presumably the leftovers from the day's business.

I hesitated for a short while, then gathered my courage and called to him in Spanish, asking if he had any food he could give me.

The moment of waiting for his reply seemed like an eternity, a vast empty space of nothing. My sad eyes watched the figure of this man disappear into the darkness of the night, and my stomach screamed. I followed the man, intent on what he did with the bag of refuse. My heart leapt as I saw him throw the bag onto a pile of similar-looking bags piled around several large bins.

I made my way towards the bins, peering over my shoulder in case anyone was watching. With trembling hands I untied the big knot of the bag the man had been carrying, and to my delight found all sorts of sandwiches wrapped in foil and a box of crispy salad. I took out the best I could find and squeezed them into my artist bag alongside my brushes. On closing the bag, an enormous feeling of humility and guilt instantly engulfed me, filled up my heart and carved terrible holes in my soul.

But the night was too cold, and I was too hungry, to reflect upon what I had become.

Pacing through the darkened streets, I finally found a bench, unpacked a packet of foil-wrapped sandwiches from my bag, and began to eat. The bread was dry at the edges and the filling was sparse and tasteless, but it felt like heaven to eat after such a long day. I struggled to swallow, due to the dryness in my throat, but I persevered until I had eaten the whole sandwich.

With a mute prayer of thanks on my lips I thanked the world for such a lavish supper, and felt warm waves of gratitude slowly embrace my sobbing heart.

CHAPTER FOUR

My summer sandals were ripped at the seams and a buckle hanging loose from one of the straps after my long trek to the town and beach. I had no choice but to walk barefoot to the market the next morning to get some another pair. How was I going to pay for it? I had no idea.

My beautiful embroidered pink dress touched the ground as I walked, so nobody saw that I walked barefoot.

I made confident steps on the pavement and felt the breath of Mother Earth push through the heavy concrete layers as the warm vibes embraced my feet, and then my whole body. I hummed a song to myself and followed the narrow road to the market.

The small gift shops opened onto the street, inviting tourists to come in and buy souvenirs. So enticing were they, that instead of going straight to the market to get the sandals, I entered one of the souvenir shops.

The shop heaved with customers, the shelves packed with all sorts of souvenirs, from exquisitely painted wooden spoons to neatly embroidered woollen flowers and dollies wearing intricately patterned dresses so beautiful I could not help but touch them, and then softly caress their beautiful plaited hair.

I sighed, closed my eyes and again was that little girl from Chelsea playing in my nanny's big rose garden. The smell of roses was so strong I could swear I was back there again. My eyes opened and I saw a little rose scented bottle on a shelf before me, and picked it up. One moment the little bottle was in my hand, and the next a shove from behind and it smashed to the floor in a million tiny pieces.

A little dose of the rose liquid spilt on my hands, and I could not help but bring them up to my face to inhale the comforting aroma.

An elderly man wearing a big apron stained with paint came from behind the counter and through the crowd towards me.

'I am so sorry,' I said. 'How much does it cost?'

'It is not your fault, señora,' he said with a nice English accent, 'I will clear it up.'

'But I dropped it, sir. I need to pay for it. How much is it? Please tell me.'

'A young lad pushed into you,' the elderly man replied. 'Young people nowadays, they no longer care about the small things. They live in a fast-paced world, do they not? They break things and they do not even notice.' The old man smiled at me, and then he continued.

'But you, young lady,' he said, 'you are so attentive, so… gentle… so…' He was trying to search for the right word. '… *different*,' he said.

I blushed and bowed down gracefully to him.

The old man smiled and took a new rose scented bottle from the shelf.

'For you,' he said, 'a gift.'

And handed it to me.

CHAPTER FIVE

After my small dinner of restaurant food leftovers, I sat on the beach and gazed at the blood orange moon. It seemed as if it spilled all its love over the sky, taking the sea in its arms, rocking it gently from side to side, accompanied by the soft shrieking lullaby of passing birds. As the night wore on, I felt a warm breeze play gently on my cheeks and I squinted. I caught the last glimpse of the seagulls soaring, flapping their mighty wings and squabbling like children. Another flock joined them and their high-pitched shrieks penetrated my ear so sweetly, vibrating throughout my entire body.

A little voice interrupted: '¡Mira arriba!' it said. '¡Mira arriba al cielo!'

I turned around and to my surprise saw the small figure of a boy. His hair was long and dark and bushy. His messy fringe fell heavily over his face. He grinned at me, the moon lighting up his round grimy cheeks and gummy smile, his eyes shining.

I did not know much Spanish, but enough to ask him if he was okay. The little boy nodded, and asked if I was okay too. I nodded in return, and smiled, and in English I told him I was completely alone, just me and the sea. He pointed to the sky with a triumphant, toothy grin, as if he understood every word I said.

'Well, yes, and the seagulls,' I said. 'How could I forget them?'

I asked him where his mummy was so late at night.

'Where all good mamas are,' the boy replied in heavily accented English, a searing, barely noticeable pain shooting across his little face causing a sudden pain in my heart like the stab of a sharp knife.

I swallowed back my tears as the little boy stood there, frowning at me.

'Please,' I said, 'tell me more about the seagulls.'

The boy's face now beamed, and he opened his mouth to speak, pointing with his filthy index finger at the seagulls:

'There, there, up. Look, madam! Look at the seagulls! Now listen, look at them and listen!'

He spoke with the enthusiasm only a child can show. My eyes followed his finger to the seagulls dancing in the night sky, and warm waves of love filled my heart. I nodded, signalling I was ready to listen to his story.

The little boy held his breath for a while, and then he opened his mouth and the words tumbled out in broken, almost perfect, English.

'Long, long time ago,' he said, 'in an unknown land, there were many people that did not want to follow the orders and the rules of the dark forces that gathered in their land sucking up all the goodness from it, wreaking havoc to pastures and killing the cattle and transforming the whole landscape. People rebelled and after their bloody mutiny a lot of leaders fighting for a good cause lost their lives. Their wives and their orphaned children wept bitterly.'

'A million clouds shed their tears in the shape of white feathers. They landed softly on the cheeks of little boys and girls who were dreaming to see their fathers and their mothers alive again.'

'As the white feathers floated to the ground the beaks, the legs, the eyes and the whole tiny bodies emerged from them at once. The newly born creatures soared upwards and loved hovering above the large gulfs, and children started to call them "gulfs", but with time omitted the "f" sound and it became "guls" and then "gulls". Very often they added the word 'sea' and eventually they called these majestic creatures "seagulls". They migrated miles and miles away and using their sense of smell could navigate and reach the most remote destinations. And that is where seagulls come from.'

The boy sighed heavily as he ended his story.

My eyes shimmered like a pair of diamonds, and I wanted to hold him tight, such was his sadness.

A wall of silence fell between us, soon broken by a sudden outburst of high- pitched shrieks above our heads.

The boy pointed upwards.

'This flock used to be in a nursery run by two bigger male seagulls in summer,' he said, the vigour now returned to his face.

I looked up and saw two smaller creatures hovering in the air following two big birds commanding them by a series of intricate movements of their flapping wings.

I looked back to the boy, hoping to learn more, but the boy was already walking silently along the beach and vanished as quickly as he had appeared.

I rubbed my eyes, wondering if what had happened was real, if the boy had been nothing but a dream. I spotted a white handkerchief with a beautifully embroidered seagull on it by my feet. It probably fell out of the pocket of the boy's trousers, I thought. I picked the handkerchief up, folded it carefully and put it into my pocket. I looked up wistfully at the seagulls again. Where before what had appeared to my eyes a squawking, chaotic mess now became a dance of life. Their shrieking told the story of their hunger, their constant battle for survival, of unborn babies, of mourning, of hours of travelling, of fatigue, of parenting, of sunsets and sunrises, of love.

Overcome with tiredness, I went back inside, headed for my little shelter made of twigs and old pieces of cloth on the beach and fell beneath my rugged blanket, dreaming of seagulls.

I woke up the next day on the beach with a terrible headache. I breathed in the fresh morning air, held it for a few seconds, then slowly exhaled till my lungs were empty. I did this a few more times but still the burden in my chest would not lift. I yearned for the soft kisses of my ex-husband, and longed terribly for the pair of loving eyes and the touch of his soft hands. For a fleeting moment I saw his face in my mind, and heard his voice pleading with me to return.

I turned around quickly, expecting him to be standing there repentant, his arms open, tears flowing down his face.

But I was alone.

I stood there in perfect stillness.

Then came the other voice, the one from nowhere and from everywhere.

Love yourself, Christina. Be your light.

I sank to the soft white sand, my eyes choked with tears.

The morning sun had burnt the clouds from the sky, and I walked along the beach, heading for the town. As I neared the marketplace, I searched the narrow, dirty streets for I knew not what. A stray cat appeared and rubbed its body against my ankles. The cat was a beautifully striped ginger tom. I stroked him for a while as he nuzzled into my hand, and felt at last I had found a friend. Then, as if he had decided on his purpose, he resumed his journey, moving steadily up the street, stopping at regular intervals to drink in the bliss of the moment.

Philip's voice came to me as if trapped behind thick glass.

'Christina, my darling, come home. Everything will be different. Please, let me feel you in my arms again.'

A fountain of tears appeared in my eyes and I followed the cat down the dirty street, pretending I could not hear. The voice was persistent, deep and penetrating, and it tore me apart.

I wandered the streets and the marketplace all day, until I heard the voice no more.

CHAPTER SIX

I awoke to sunrays dancing on my face and the faint sounds of the market coming to life a little way off.

I smelt fresh doughnuts. My soul rejoiced at the beauty of the morning, my body, however shrank from the coldness of the night. My blanket was ripped and needed a wash and my face and my hands were covered with the dust from the streets. I grabbed my bag with my painting toolkit and marched towards the market.

When I arrived at the market, I found it already bending under the weight of products being unloaded and stalls being put up. My eyes found it hard to embrace it all: the food, the toys, the books (new and second-hand), old magazines, paintings, postcards, jewellery, kitchen utensils, clothes, handbags, fresh flowers, fruit and vegetables.

As I wandered through the market, looking for a spot for myself to set up, a strong smell of fresh bread wafted towards me. I turned to where it was coming from and saw a stall piled high with all sorts of beautifully shaped bread loaves, attended by an elderly lady.

'Good morning!' I said, and smiled.

The elderly lady looked into my eyes and then at my ragged dress, and I became suddenly conscious of what I must look like, and what she might say. But her faced beamed.

'And what a beautiful morning it is, my darling!' she said, producing a little tray laden with thick slices of bread with what looked like some sort of brown topping. 'Please help yourself, my dear. Home-made bread and fig marmalade. It is delicious.'

I grabbed a slice from the tray and devoured the bread and marmalade ravenously.

'I am afraid I have no money to pay you,' I said, utterly ashamed.

'My darling,' the elderly lady said kindly, 'I did not ask you to pay. I may be blind in one eye, but I can see clearly with the other one. And what I see is a beautiful soul in need. Please, help yourself to more bread. Actually, I will pack for you a few slices together with a small pot of marmalade.'

I blushed again, and looked at my dress, having no words to say to such kindness.

The old lady smiled, took my hands in hers, and said: 'You are very blessed with your hands.' Her eyes fixated on the paint stain on my dress.

She looked like she wanted to embrace and comfort me, as if I were her own little child.

'I had better go now,' I said, forcing a smile. 'Will you be here tomorrow?'

'I am here every day, my darling,' the old lady replied.

The old lady looked deep into my eyes, and waved goodbye.

I knew what I had to do now. I had to find a spot for myself and start painting as soon as possible so I could repay the kindness of the bread lady.

I wandered through the stalls, the colours of chocolate covered candies mingling with the scent of flowers, the gentle clacking of hand-made wooden toys on strings swaying in the light breeze. My eyes spotted a blue ballerina doll on a souvenir stall. The vivid expression of her face mesmerised me. I touched her beautiful dress and her soft hands.

'Hands,' I murmured to myself, and put down the doll. I examined my own hands.

'Oh God,' I uttered quietly, with quivering lips, 'I thank you for my hands. I promise you that whatever these hands touch they will turn into miracles. Oh, I promise you. This is what I owe you, to spread the magic of your invisible heartfelt presence and shape beautifully all things around me. Such is your will.'

With my hands still shaking, I made a sign of 'Amen' and closed my eyes. I placed my hands on my heart and felt it thump with a new-found purpose.

I found a place to set up my canvas on the very edge of the market, my solitary figure – a tiny dot marked in the vast universe.

Sunrays jumped playfully on my cheeks, dazzling my eyes. I moved to the shade of a big tree, its leaves like a massive crown protecting my body from the scorching heat, and sat there mixing my paint.

The people passing by paid me no attention at all, and I began to paint.

I had much to say to this world.

CHAPTER SEVEN

The beach was calm, hardly anyone was there. Golden sunrays spilled onto the sea. I heard music, and I didn't know where it came from. I turned my head and saw the seagulls dancing madly in the air. Their shrieking echoed in my soul. I placed my hand on my heart. I felt pain. I wanted to faint. I wanted to see that boy again. His stories embraced my heart and I sank deeply into the ocean of his love. His almond-shaped dark eyes were like a deep well, and I wanted to dive in and measure his depths.

I returned to the same spot as yesterday to find that boy, but he was not there. I looked up at the sky. Oh, how I wanted to fly, to soar up into the sky with the seagulls, to feel the gentle breeze on my face.

'Oh, God,' I whispered, and then I collapsed.

When I opened my eyes, I saw the face of a man. His hands affectionately touched mine.

'¿Estás bien?' he asked.

I nodded. The man quickly stood up and nervously rubbed his hands. I was sure I had seen these eyes before. He didn't say a word, he just stared at me.

'What's your name?' I asked.

'I am Martin,' he said, blushing fiercely.

'I am Christina,' I said.

The smell of his perfume floated in the air.

He took a deep breath and stretched his hand.

'I will help you to stand up, if you don't mind.'

As he was helping me to stand up, I found myself kneeling before him. This time it was my turn to blush. I turned my face away, every part of me trembling. His strong hand helped me keep my balance, and he pulled me to my feet, leaving me still wondering what had happened.

'You lost your consciousness,' he said, as if reading my mind.

I looked at his eyes and took a few steps away from him.

'You are English, Christina?' he said.

I nodded. 'And you?'

His hands in his pockets now, he smiled.

'Well,' he said, seeming unable to meet my gaze, 'that's complicated.'

I stared at him, my head too fuzzy to understand what he was saying.

'I will take you home,' he said, and offered me his hand.

But something told me I needed to get away from this man. I gave him a faint smile, and said: 'Thank you for your help.'

And I turned and strode away quickly till the figure of the man became a little dot and finally disappeared. It was then that I stopped, took a deep breath and looked up at the sun shining over the sea. There is not a single creature in this world that would not stop to drink in this scenery. I spotted a flock of seagulls. Transfixed by this magical ritual of natural forces, they flapped their wings and made a big circle saluting the sun. I remembered the little boy. Oh God! How I wanted to see him and hear one of his magical stories again.

I plodded along the beach, then took the stairs and crossed the street to the market. At the corner of the market, I saw a little bent figure wrapped in a shawl standing behind the bread stall. His curly dark hair fell on his forehead. His almond-shaped eyes looked me up and down. It was him – the Seagull Boy.

The smell of bread captivated my mind and my soul. I wanted to join in its mad dance, how I wanted to be a part of it. Oh, how I wanted, but then the boy's face staring at me brought me back to the ground. I felt my bare feet rooted in the warm pavement and my eyes widened.

'Hello. Do you remember me?' I whispered to the boy.

'Yep,' he said. 'How are you doing, madam?'

He stretched his hand to shake mine.

'I am Christina,' I said, and smiled faintly.

The little boy smiled back, and I stood there, waiting in anticipation for him to tell me his name. Almost a minute passed, and he remained silent.

'Are you not going to tell me your name?' I said eventually.

The boy's grin now spread right across his face, and his almond eyes widened and sparkled.

'Names are labels,' he said, 'and I am not a label.'

'I have never thought about it like that,' I said. 'Well, then, I will not be a label either.'

I giggled at the wisdom of such a young boy, and put my hands in my pockets to check if there was enough change from the sale of one of my paintings to buy some bread. I took out three euros.

'Can I have one medium-size loaf with olives and one small with figs and raisins please, oh wise one?'

The small boy wrapped the loaves of bread in a newspaper with dexterous hands, and I handed him the money. The bread smelled so good, I pulled back the wrapping a little and tasted a mouthful of the olive loaf.

'This is amazing!' I said.

'My nanny's bread is the best!' said the boy. 'And the fig jam. She has been unwell lately, so she cannot make as many things as she used to. But at least she still is able to make bread.'

The boy's face grew sullen and his body shrank in the cold wind.

'Oh, I am so sorry for your nanny being unwell,' I said. 'I wish her good health. She must be so proud of such a clever grandson.'

'I am just helping her to make ends meet. It is our sole income. The bread business is not easy nowadays. Some loaves go to the local shops and we also sell them in the market, and some...' He hesitated a while, and then said, 'I never want to waste a single crumb.'

He pointed now at the seagulls dancing madly in the wind.

'They eat anything, but the crust of a stale bread is their delicacy. They are the best recycling and cleaning factory in the world.'

I frowned, not quite following what he had said. 'What do you mean?'

'Seagulls,' he said, triumphantly. 'They eat all the leftovers of Spain. They eat all the leftovers of the world.'

'It seems like you are a little expert on seagulls and their lives.'

'My granddaddy taught me everything,' he said, then cleared his throat as if he had something important to say.

'Once upon a time...'

I placed my hand on my heart and I blinked, readying myself for one of his beautiful stories.

'...there was a sea monster living in Gran Canaria. If anyone approached the beach the sea monster would catch them, and smash them his gigantic hands. Once, a seagull stopped on the beach and said to him *I will save all the people from the beaches of Gran Canaria.* The monster laughed.'

I laughed as well, wondering how a tiny seagull could save the people from the hands of such a giant.

The boy continued: '*I challenge you,* said the seagull, *to eat as many leftovers in the landfills of Gran Canaria as you can, and then my flock and I will do the same. Whoever eats the biggest amount will rule the beach, and whoever eats the smallest amount will leave the beach forever.*'

'Wow,' I said, 'and what did the monster say to that?'

The boy carried on: 'The monster laughed and laughed and he put a crown of seaweed on his head, and said: *That I am a ruler here is as obvious as the sky is blue.* Then he gave a mighty roar and laughed again. The next day, the flock of seagulls gathered near the landfills with shrieks and mighty cries.'

'And then what happened?' I asked.

'They ate so much their bellies could hardly find the space for any more food. And they beat the monster.'

'And the monster?'

'He was so ashamed he left the island, never to be seen again. The people of the island placed white lilies on the edge of the sea as a token of gratitude to the seagulls. Then they danced and prayed to the God of the sun, and watched the seagulls glide into the air and form a beautiful circle in the sky. Their shrieking and mighty cries echoed in the people's ears. The seagull babies sipped from the water's edge as their proud parents flew high above. People bathed in the sea and laughter filled the air. Since that time all the beaches around Gran Canaria belong to the seagulls.'

The boy wiped his mouth, and said: 'Well, that's the end. I'd better go now.'

He started packing away.

'Shall I help you?' I said.

'Thank you, ma'am,' replied the boy. 'I can manage by myself. If you happen to look for me in the market one day and cannot find me, just ask anyone here for *las gaviotas*. They will know who you mean.'

The boy shoved his bag into a basket attached to the back of his bike, waved me goodbye and rode off before I could say anything.

I returned to the beach, took out a small box of olives, tomatoes and the bread I had bought from the boy, and started my lunch. The wind carried the song of nearby children closer and closer...

'One seagull floats in the wind.
It dreams, oh, it has dreams
of a yummy fish,
roasted peppers.
Ah, sweet, sweet.

Two seagulls circle the shore.
They cry, oh they cry.
No bread crumbs, no more.
Ah, caw, caw.

Three seagulls swimming in the sea
catch a mighty fish.
It's gone, gone.

Soggy chips washed ashore
will fill up bellies.
They rumble, rumble.

Four seagulls dance over their prey
mighty supper will be there,
will be there.'

I rocked gently to and fro, my feet beating out the rhythm of the words on the sand. Innocence spread its wings on the sky, I saw its formless body from the distance and two huge seagulls landed in front of me, the greedy look in their eyes causing my hands to tremble.

'Here you are,' I said, and scattered a handful of breadcrumbs before me on the beach.

The two seagulls packed their beaks with as many crumbs as they had the capacity for, and flew away.

The day began to sink in a melody of song and the sky above grew darker and darker.

There was a storm approaching.

I could feel it.

I had no home.

Where the hell was Marina when I needed her most?

CHAPTER EIGHT

Weeks went by. Nights were long. I suffered from insomnia. I was scared to death. I was scared of being robbed again.

But robbed of what? I was a poor street artist. I had nothing of value. Nothing apart from my painting toolkit and the canvas I bought for the coins found in the pockets of my skirt.

The streets at night were full of unsavoury people, drunkards and beggars. People carried knives these days. I could be found dead the next day in an alley somewhere, my throat cut or my heart stabbed through or my entire body sliced up like a piece of meat.

Would it make any difference?

I had been stabbed through the heart so many times in my life, anyway. A broken home, a bitter divorce, time spent locked up in a mental hospital.

Who could bear all that and be normal?

My sanity lay in the hands of my creativity. My life depended on my art.

Whenever I earned a bit of money on my paintings, the first thing I bought was more paint to make sure I had enough for another painting, and another canvas to paint on.

Crazy, isn't it?

I hadn't had a nice breakfast or supper in my stomach for weeks. Very often I prioritized a shower in the swimming pool over food. I paid for the access to the pool, but I never used it, only the shower. I couldn't stand being dirty for a long period of time. These days hunger was something I had got used to. When you know you are not going to eat regularly, sooner or later your body becomes more relaxed.

Some days, however, it was all too much. Everything in me screamed. I wanted to be back home. London appeared to be a paradise compared to this island. I felt trapped. I had no money for the flight. I had forgotten Marina's phone number and had no idea where she lived. I could wait for her to find me, I guess. But what if she was not even here anymore, and moved back to Peru with her husband for good?

What then?

I could wait or act. In order to retain the remnants of the dignity I had left, I chose to act.

I kept going to the market to sell my paintings, and to paint more. Each day was a rush as I had to reach the artist market before sunrise or there would be no space. I would place my canvas in front of me and to take out my paint.

One morning, when I had everything assembled, I felt someone's eyes on me.

I looked up.

'Good morning,' the man said, a broad smile across his face. 'How are you?'

'I am not too bad,' I said, 'But I think we bump into each other too often.'

He giggled. My eyes fixed on my canvas. My fingers were hungry for the touch of paint. My soul needed it badly. Martin said something else to me, and I nodded. I didn't know what he said.

My art had always been my true mother, placing its warm hands around my waist and comforting my soul. My art was my friend chatting with me in the lonely world. My art, oh, my art.

I placed my finger on my lips. 'So, what do you want?' I asked.

His eyes wide open, he gazed at me. 'Well, a good chat with a neighbour is always very welcome, here in Spain.'

'I know nothing about your Spanish rules,' I said. 'What I do know is that I need peace and quiet to focus on my painting.'

I ground the words through my teeth. His face was like a wounded dog. He dropped his head and marched away.

'Now,' I grumbled, 'I can focus on my painting.'

This thumping heart of mine had always wanted something, and now I promised to never let it down. I finished my painting in two hours and placed it with the others around me.

'What a nice collection,' said a man passing by.

But he did not buy anything.

Street art is not an easy business. I hardly earned money so far and hardly ate these days, relying on the kindness of strangers. How could I carry on like this? A woman of forty years in the streets? My heart thumped. On that day, I sold nothing.

It was time for some advice. This couldn't go on. I remembered the old man from the souvenir shop near the market, and I thought it would be good to visit him.

I wandered the picturesque alleys, looking around for his shop and smelling doughnuts, churros, empanadas… the smells of these floating in the air and leading my senses in a magical dance. Due to the lack of food, I started to lose my consciousness again. I leaned against a wall and managed to keep my balance.

You can't give up now, you can't. There are still so many hills to climb.

I sighed heavily and I started walking again. With slow, steady movements I dragged myself to the souvenir shop.

I saw the old man smiling to his customers, selling a beautiful dolly to one of them. Once he saw me, he let the other shop assistant take care of the customer, and he rushed towards me, offering his hand.

'I didn't think you would still remember me,' he said.

I smiled faintly. He stretched his hand towards me.

'Gustavo,' he said. 'My name is Gustavo Jose Rivero.'

'How poetic,' I said. 'I love your name, Mr Rivero. I am Christina,' I cleared my throat, and shook his hand, 'Christina Bovary.'

'Mucho gusto,' Mr Rivero said, and lifted up my hand and kissed it.

How gentlemanly, I thought.

'Please,' he said, 'do not hesitate to call me Gustavo.'

'Okay, Mr Riv— I mean Gustavo.'

He grinned, and said: 'How are you doing?'

Tears filled my eyes.

'Oh, my sweetheart. What happened?'

I looked around at all the people in the shop.

'Please come to my...we need to talk, I think,' Gustavo said.

In seconds I found myself in the back room of the shop. I looked around and saw messy shelves packed with paint, canvas, paint brushes and oil paintings.

'You look so sad.' the souvenir shop owner said.

He smiled in a warm fatherly manner.

My throat would not let the words pass as I tried to articulate what I wanted to say. With the stream of tears trickling down my cheeks I finally managed to utter: 'I just need help.'

I told him my story, how I found myself in Gran Canaria, my love of painting, and my current circumstances.

'Let me see your paintings,' he said.

I laid my paintings out for him, my heart jumping, thinking he might be interested in purchasing one.

I saw his eyes were wet as he looked at my pictures. He applied a beautiful floral handkerchief to each eye in turn, and then dabbed his cheeks.

'You remind me of an idea that I came up with a long time ago, but never found time for.'

I looked at him, puzzled.

'I have always wanted to set up a workshop to teach people to paint,' he said. He paused for the longest time, as if deep in thought, then suddenly said: 'They will take place here. And you will run them.'

'Me?' I asked, biting my upper lip, utterly confused.

'Yes,' he said, and he smiled triumphantly.

I rubbed my eyes. I couldn't believe it. I was to run painting workshops? But how? I had never done anything like this before. I cleared my throat: 'Excuse me, sir… Gustavo. But how could I – a beggar from the street – run workshops?'

The tears trimmed down my cheeks. I buried my face in my hands, and couldn't stop crying.

Gustavo left me for a few minutes, and returned, his face beaming with kindness.

'Here you are,' he said in a very soft voice. 'Buy yourself some food and some nice clothes. Also, we will think how to help you to find a home for yourself.'

'Thank you so much,' I said. 'How can I repay you for your kindness?'

'Well, I think it is me who needs to repay the world for the kindness it has offered me.' Tears came to his eyes. 'Now, go, go and turn this money into a good use. You will start your workshops as soon as possible.'

Trembling from head to toe, I left the shop.

Outside, the sun was going down.

My eyes fixated on its glowing body.

The sky blushed.

I felt love in the air.

Next morning, I returned to the shop to thank Gustavo. Tears of happiness sprang to my eyes when I saw him behind his counter serving his customers. His appearance assumed a new quality. A strange, yet beautiful, light emanated from his eyes. He raised his eyebrows and spotted me standing in the corner of his shop.

'It is so good to see you,' he said.

'Mr Rivero? I …' but the words got stuck in my throat. 'I mean, Gustavo.'

'Yes, Christina?'

'I can't find words for your kindness. Muchas gracias por todo,' I mumbled in Spanish.

'De nada mi chiquita, de nada,' he replied, and laughed wholeheartedly.

I smiled.

'Now, my dear,' he said, clearing his throat, 'we need to find you a home. I have a friend who sells the bread in the market. She knows so many people here, and might be able to help.'

I blushed at his kindness, and saw the sadness in his eyes.

'You can't stay on the streets,' he continued. 'One as delicate as you has no place there. You could stay at my house for a while, if you would like. It is warm and it would give you a roof over your head until you found something else.'

This man was so kind, but I could not accept his offer.

'I am a respectable woman,' I said, blushing, 'and you are a kind man. It would not do. People might talk.'

'I didn't mean anything, Christina,' the old man hurriedly replied. 'I was just trying to help.'

Gustavo wiped way the tears forming in his eyes.

He turned his attention to a gentleman stacking the shelves at the back of the shop.

'¡Marco!' he called. '¡Marco!'

Moments later, Marco had stopped stacking the shelves, and was busy serving customers, and Gustavo had politely bade me goodbye, and left.

CHAPTER NINE

The day came slowly, stretching itself like a cat after a good sleep under a magic starred sky. I looked to the heavens and asked the questions in my heart to God and to myself. A million doubts churned inside my mind and a million unanswered questions bathed in the sea of my restless soul.

When is the beginning of our life? Is it when we are in our mother's womb or when we start loving life itself, appreciating every minute of it? And what is life about? Is it about living for others or realizing your own dreams? Or is it a combination of both?

When flowers start to bloom, they just bloom. And the world is in awe of them, the little voice said.

My knees trembled and tears ran down my skinny cheeks.

Gustavo, as he promised, spoke to his friend, the bread lady. The bread lady's name was Sofía. Sofía, it transpired, had a friend who, in turn, happened to be a friend of Marina's and had a spare key to Marina's cottage. Sofía managed to get hold of the key, and gave it to Gustavo. She told Gustavo that Marina and her husband had returned to Peru to help her bedridden mother-in-law, and would be gone for some time.

Gustavo told me I could have the cottage for as long as I pleased. Marina, he said, would want it that way, he was sure.

I couldn't wait to see the cottage when Gustavo handed me the keys. My short, very painful, episode of homelessness, it seemed, had come to an end. And so I dragged my ripped bag with the few belongings I had left in the world to the beach where the cottage was.

I lifted my long blue skirt and raced along the sand to the foot of the stairs to my new home.

I closed my eyes and felt the soft kisses of Philip, his beard gently tickling my neck, then I opened my eyes and the memory of Philip splintered into nothing.

Inside, the cottage was as small as I had imagined, but there was still a bit of space to move around. There was a small kitchen and lounge area, and at the back a bathroom and bedroom. It was everything I needed. On the left as I entered the bedroom stood a small wardrobe and on the right a bed with a beautifully embroidered duvet and a night table beside it with a fuchsia pink art deco lamp of an unusual shape. I laid down my bag containing my life possessions on the bed. My legs trembled with exhaustion.

After unpacking my things, I headed outside for a view of the restless sea. Even though November had cooled the sand, I suddenly sensed a feeling of joyful liberation as the ocean waves invited me to play.

I danced amongst the waves, giggling like a little girl, knowing I was about to step into the most wonderful of dreams. Then a sharp squeeze of reality pulled at my heart and shattered it all. I was alone. I was alone in a foreign country with nothing but a few clothes, my painting equipment, and the dream of a better life. What on earth was I doing?

I closed my eyes.

If the world of beautiful dreams is inside you, Christina, enter this world.

'Who are you?' I shouted. 'Who are you?'

I was with you before you were born, Christina. I will be with you after you pass, and every moment in between.

Through my accelerated heartbeat I heard the voice again.

Christina, relax. Listen to your heart.

I opened my eyes.

I stopped playing with the waves and ran as fast as I could to my little cottage, and threw myself on the bed.

Gustavo had made sure the fridge and the kitchen cupboards were full, and that my wardrobe had several changes of clothes. I put on one of the new dresses, and had a bite of a blue cheese with olives and lettuce and a sip of orange juice.

I walked through the forest to the town. The music of pine trees filled my soul, the fresh scent played on my nose and teased it gently. My spirit floated and merged with the spirit of the forest.

There is no division, no separation. Everything and everyone grows from the warm womb of Mother Earth. All are part of her beautiful masterpiece called life.

I felt a little pain in my heart, squeezed my hands and held my breath.

'Sometimes I want to feel nothing,' I murmured.

How is it possible?

'To cease to exist. Just for a while.'

Then you would be dead. The dead are the stream of endless consciousness embracing everything and everyone.

'You talk in a way I do not understand,' I said, and the voice quietened.

I bit my lower lip. My heartbeat accelerated, and I continued walking through the forest listening to the bird songs.

The street soon appeared, and the first cars passed. I covered my nose so as not to breathe in the exhaust fumes. I walked down the alley and reached the souvenir shop. Gustavo was in his usual good mood. When he saw me, he grinned and beckoned me inside to the back room in which we last spoke.

All the shelves were tidy, and the painting equipment was tucked away in a box in the corner.

'There,' Gustavo pointed at a huge desk, 'for you.'

My eyes shone. It was beautiful. A fresh bouquet of flowers was in the vase, sitting on the corner of the desk.

There were drawing pads, canvas, watercolour, oil paint, chalk, pencils, and many other artistic paraphernalia. My jaw dropped, then I clapped my hands. A tear rolled down my cheek.

'I… I don't know how to thank you. I…' my voice broke.

'This is your studio, Christina,' he said. 'You will run your workshops here.'

He bowed gracefully.

'I…'

The words remained stuck in my throat. It seemed they always did at moments like this.

'The first students should be arriving soon,' Gustavo said.

I took out my paint and brushes from my bag, and set them by the easel already set up for me.

And I waited.

The clock struck five. The first participants were supposed to be here by now.

'We have time,' I murmured to myself, and went over to sit in the big cosy chair in the corner.

After a while I peeped at my watch. Half an hour had passed. My hands started sweating, and my heart thumped.

Then I heard a familiar voice from within the shop.

'Good afternoon. I am so sorry to be late. I got stuck at work.'

'Please enter,' I heard Gustavo say. 'The artist is waiting.'

The door opened, and there stood Martin. He grinned at me and then dropped his head.

'Well I know I was not welcome last time we met, but I heard about your workshops and I couldn't resist.'

'You couldn't resist what?' I shot back in a cold tone, my cheeks burning.

'I mean… I mean I couldn't resist trying my hand at painting,' Martin mumbled.

'Well, nobody's turned up,' I said, 'so I guess the workshop today is cancelled.'

Gustavo appeared at Martin's side.

'You are very welcome to stay, Martin,' he said. 'Christina, please just start your class with your student.'

'Okay,' I said, and grabbed my brush. 'A one-to-one class it is, then.'

My hand trembled as I grabbed my brush – whether from rage or from something else, I do not know – and the brush slipped out of my fingers and clattered to the floor.

I knelt down to get the brush, and so did Martin. I felt his hot breath on my cheeks and then suddenly the warmth of his lips landing on mine like a thousand rose petals caressed by the sun. I quickly turned my face away from him.

'We shouldn't–'

'And tell me why we shouldn't?' he said. 'Why shouldn't we kiss?'

For the first time, I saw him angry. I shook my head.

'I see the sparkles dancing in your eyes,' Martin said. 'They are saying yes to life and love. So why are your lips uttering these words? Why are they defying the language of these beautiful eyes?'

His own eyes were wet now.

'I don't need anyone,' I said, trying to compose myself. 'I am happy the way I am.'

'So why do you tremble every time I come close to you? Why do you blush every time our breath meets in a dance?'

His eyes burned fiercely, begging for my attention.

But I was not ready for it.

'Go,' I said. 'Please, go.'

But he would not.

'Do your scars from the past open and bleed?' he said. 'We all have those scars, Christina.'

'Please go, Martin,' I said softly.

'You see, you don't even have an answer. I can hear your heart wrenching at the pain of you trying to suppress your feelings. Tell me. What do you feel?'

'Martin, what you are talking about are sacred things that happen between a man and woman. I do not think that I am ready. Let us just be friends.'

At these words, Martin handed my brush to me, breathing deep as he did so.

'I can wait,' he said.

'I am afraid that I will never be ready,' I replied.

My hands trembled as the tears came to his eyes. I offered my trembling hand to him and we cried in each other's arms like two lost children.

CHAPTER TEN

On my way home from the souvenir shop I stopped, removed my shawl and let the evening put its cool, misty arms around my neck. I breathed deep and listened to my heartbeat. More tears trickled down my face, and I heard a mighty shrill in the sky.

I looked up and saw a circle of seagulls floating in the air, and then form a line, and fly eastwards. I gazed at them as they slowly disappeared from my view.

Birds fly as high and as far as they can, their navigation system never fails. Why wouldn't we trust our own internal navigation system that leads us to the paths in our lives? Why wouldn't we think we can fly better than the seagulls?

I closed my eyes and felt a twinge in my back. My heart throbbed. In my mind I painted Martin's beautiful face and the light radiating from it.

That night stretched like a dark tunnel. I didn't want to go through it and desperately looked for the light. I switched on my fuchsia lamp. The room was bright again. I looked at the mirror and spotted two lines on my forehead.

'Where have these years gone?' I said to the night.

Tears appeared in my eyes and I swallowed my saliva.

'All my best years were taken by a man that couldn't make me happy. Now I find a beautiful soul, and it is too late. I cannot love again. I can't.'

My voice broke into sobs which grew louder and louder.

I took a deep breath. The silence fell on my puffy eyes, and I fell asleep.

I dreamt of big dark eyes, a fire burning within, pleasant and warm. I climbed inside those eyes, and the fire did not burn my skin. A beautiful light drew me in deeper. I found myself dancing inside the huge eyes and felt a warm wave of love. I wondered who these eyes belonged to. Then I jumped out of them and the whole face appeared.

The face of Martin.

CHAPTER ELEVEN

I opened my eyes to watch the mysterious painter spread the paint upon the sky. Pink coloured canvas of the day. My senses bathed in the explosion of love.

The swarm of round-bellied bees entered the cottage through the tiny slot of an open window. A sweet nectar of summer days filled the air even though Mother Earth was beginning to adorn her body with gold and orange. I sank into the tapestry of colours in my mind and gradually wandered off from thoughts of yesterday. This moment of bliss and the awareness of the sheer abundance of life danced in my body, nourishing each cell and rejuvenating my entire being.

I placed my hands on my heart and uttered a prayer of gratitude.

A soft music sounded from outside. I opened the window and set the door ajar, causing the music to stream into my cottage. A tiny figure wrapped in a shawl stood on my threshold, bending under the heaviness of a large basket.

'¡Hola!' a cracking voice came from the shapeless figure, pulling the shawl from his face to reveal filthy cheeks with charming dimples.

'¡Hola!' I replied, my eyes wide open.

Of course, it was the Seagull Boy, his dark eyes looked at me shyly.

'I wondered if I should knock,' he said, 'but the door was open.'

'Hello my little Seagull Boy, how nice to see you.'

His face beamed when he heard how I called him.

I stretched out my hand and he shook it gracefully.

'I can be anything,' he said proudly, and counted off each name on his fingers as he said it. 'They call me a bread boy, a sea monster, the one who runs after seagulls, a freak…'

'I really like the one who runs after seagulls,' I said.

'Would you like some fresh bread, madam? See, now I am the bread boy. I am running from one house to another selling this bread for my grandma.'

'How nice to help your grandma, but it is not Saturday.'

'Yes, I know.'

'You should be in school, young man,' I whispered.

'Animals don't go to schools and they live their lives.'

Big eyes stared at me.

'Well,' I said, 'you are a child and you need to go to school.'

'Animal babies learn from parents. They do not need school.'

'You are not an animal.'

He grinned.

'And how do you know?'

We both burst into laughter, and I told him I would take two loaves of bread as I was expecting guests tonight.

'Guests?' he said.

'I meant my students. I would love to share some of this yummy bread with them tonight at my workshop.'

'Oh, I see,' he said, 'so you are a teacher. No wonder you talk about school.'

'No, I am just a painter who has started running a sort of painting club.'

His face changed.

'You are a painter? Wow! Could you paint a bird for me, please? I can't pay you, but I can give you an extra loaf of bread, if you want.'

He grinned at me again.

'Of course I can,' I said. 'You don't have to give me anything. Just tell me one of your beautiful stories. I have never heard anything like them before. Where did you get them?'

'I heard them from my grandpa. Some I made up by myself.'

'Where is your grandpa? I would love to meet him and listen to his stories as well.'

His eyes glistened and he dropped his head.

'He passed away some time ago.'

'Oh, I am so sorry to hear that. I…'

I felt the words get stuck in my throat. I could not continue.

'My grandpa used to tell me stories,' the boy said. 'Now I tell his stories.'

The voice inside me stirred. The words for me alone.

Memories of the dead flow in beautiful stories once conjured up by sacred mouths.

'And your parents?' I asked.

'They died too.'

'Oh, I am so sorry, I had no idea.'

I watched as small tears danced in his eyes, ready to run free down his cheeks. With one movement of his hand the Seagull Boy wiped his eyes, and the tears disappeared.

'I am so sorry,' I said.

'Don't. It is life. I remember when my mum and dad died. I cried and cried.'

Tears swept down my cheeks.

The Seagull Boy continued:

'The seagulls came and sat on the roof of our house and cried too. Their shriek filled up the air. The clouds grew darker. The whole world cried that day. Rain washed our wounds, but the scars remain forever.'

He took a deep breath and then closed his mouth. I gave him a big hug.

Then he said, 'I bet you must have lost your parents too.'

'Why do you think so?' I asked.

'You are always by yourself. I saw you in the summer hanging around in the streets.'

'My parents are alive but live in a different country. I came to Spain on my own.'

I don't know why I lied to him.

'They are in a different country?' His eyes opened in wonder. 'Why don't they come here so you will be happier?'

'Things are not always easy as you think. I just told them I was going to visit my friend.' I paused. 'But things changed. I lost my life savings. I couldn't find my friend. I was left in the streets. My parents had no idea I was homeless.'

He looked at me.

'But you have a nice place now. I am happy for you,' he said.

'Yes, now I have. But the place is not everything. The most important thing is what you carry in your heart. Mine was empty and drained. I didn't feel at home with it. I suppose I was homeless before, even with a roof over my head.'

'And now?'

'And now I do not know.'

'My grandpa used to say: All the treasures are locked in our hearts. I always wondered what it meant.'

My eyes scrutinized his face as if he was the biggest riddle in the world. I sighed and said: 'I know you don't want to tell me your name, but at least tell me your age.'

'I will tell you because you are my special friend.'

He grinned and I felt such warmth embracing my heart.

'I am ten,' he said.

My eyes gazed at him. 'You are very mature for ten.'

'When you don't have parents, you need to be your own mum and dad. I have only granny now and her health is… not good. One day I will be by myself…' and his voice broke down.

We both froze at the heaviness of these words.

An eerie silence filled the room.

When the Seagull Boy left, I gathered my brushes, my canvas, and my paints and marched straight to the shop for the class. Part of me did not want to meet Martin, but my heart trembled at the thought of him being there. I felt warm waves like an entire ocean embracing my body and my soul.

When I arrived at the souvenir shop I went straight to the studio. Martin was there. Alone. Just Martin.

I sat at the table.

'Hello!' he said.

I dropped my eyes.

'I didn't come to pester you, I…' he said, 'I wanted to apologize.'

'It is okay.'

'No, it isn't. I kissed you and told you about too many things while in fact we should have been discussing painting techniques.'

'Thank you,' I said.

He took out his notebook and drawing pad, and I began the lesson. He looked at me and grinned.

'When you have shown me all these painting techniques, I will be able to paint. I wouldn't even dare to try to be good as you but, at least I will be able to paint.'

'There is something bigger than just techniques,' I told him.

'What is that?'

'Passion. Passion is the first thing you need to learn about painting. Passion dances in your soul, filling it up with the beautiful energy of love. Your soul spills this love onto the canvas, and that is how you paint. If you feel it – this passion, this love – others will feel it. It is a sort of divine energy. The canvas you paint on is the canvas of your life.'

I said all this in one gulp, and realized I knew nothing about this man.

'So, Martin,' I said, 'tell me about your passion.'

Martin looked at the ceiling, then at me and gently patted his chin. I tried to guess what was happening inside his mind and heart, and behind his half-closed, faraway eyes. The silence didn't last long, as it was interrupted by a strong gust of wind howling outside.

'I save animals from bad conditions,' he eventually said. 'If they are old or unwanted, the only solution for them is either euthanasia or the slaughterhouse.'

Large tears fell on his cheeks.

'That is terrible,' I said. 'Those poor creatures.'

'You can't understand, dear Christina, till you see it. I have been there. When I was studying to be a vet, they sent us to these places to alert us to the practice and the hygiene of such establishments, and the legislation involved. We were sent to these places of death, just for us to be able to help animals later. Isn't it weird?'

'It is,' I said, nervously fiddling with the ripped pocket of my jeans skirt.

'You see them being killed for a piece of meat and then you know everything about them. Their guts basically. Most of all, I learnt some animals cannot be saved. In these places, I learnt how to end the suffering of animals whose condition was beyond hope.'

'You are such a gift to the world, Martin,' I said.

Martin smiled through his tears.

'I am only a voice for animals,' he said, 'the voice that they don't have.'

At the sound of the word 'voice' something uneasy shifted inside me. Animals obviously do not have voices. Who can speak for them if not a human being?

'But how about human beings? We have a voice. We can express easily our annoyance when we feel our boundaries are being trespassed by others. Our grand brain processes the information but sometimes fails to process it properly, if at all. The voice we have is very often one we do not use. Is that not true as well, Martin?'

Martin looked at me, his eyes full of wonder. His hands trembled and he put them in the pockets of his green trousers, and closed his eyes. There was sweat on his forehead.

Oh, how I wanted to kiss that sweet forehead, and I blushed at the thought.

My heart accelerated.

Forehead kisses are meant for friends, aren't they?

I rose on my feet to reach Martin's forehead, planted a big kiss upon it. My lips felt his hot skin. I pressed my cold hands against his forehead to check if he had a fever. It reminded me of my days as a nurse checking the condition of patients. I often acted like a nurse still, checking my pulse, the colour of my tongue, even examining other people's faces in search of symptoms without them even knowing.

All total madness.

Martin opened his eyes and mouth, and lifted up his brush.

We chatted for a while.

'Now I am ready to follow your instructions, my teacher,' he said.

We tried brush strokes and drawing contours of distant figures. There was grandeur in the silence of these moments. Something my mind could not grasp, but my eager heart felt it.

CHAPTER TWELVE

The night was long. I had a dream that Gustavo and Martin ran away from me, in spite of how I shouted at them at the top of my lungs to come back. I ran after them, but I could not find them. Then I saw the whole figure of a man, his face deformed, stretching his arm towards me. I cried and ran from him as fast as I could.

I woke up, sweating and I rushed to the souvenir shop without eating breakfast. My heart pounded and my blood galloped like wild horses in my veins. I reached the souvenir shop to see a crowd of people gathering around the cordoned street, and I saw police with dogs. With tears in my eyes, I pushed my way through the crowd and saw the smashed windows of the souvenir shop. I saw a broken doll on the pavement in front of the shop. The owner was not there.

'Excuse me, what is happening here?' I asked one of the strangers from the crowd, my heart nearly reaching my throat.

The lady turned to me. I saw a terror in her face.

'My darling, bad things, bad things.'

She shook her head and, swallowing her tears, blurted out: 'They broke into the souvenir shop yesterday.'

'Who is *they*?' I asked.

'We don't know yet. The police are investigating now.'

'And the owner? I mean Mr Rivero. Where is he?'

The lady broke into tears. 'He is in hospital.'

Tears of rage exploded from my eyes.

'What the hell is going on? Did they hurt him?' I yelled.

But the woman was too distraught to answer.

I looked at the crowd of people, at the smashed windows, at how the policemen grimaced and the police dogs barked. The world spun around me. I hardly managed to keep my balance. I felt my soul tearing itself apart. I turned around looking for familiar faces – but there were none.

I had to get away from here. I could stand it no longer. I ran, frightened, towards my cottage to change my clothes, then to the seashore, and the endless, restless sea.

The cool water embraced my waist and arms and reached my shoulder. The waves turned into the warm loving hands I was missing. My tears joined the saltiness of the sea, and the stones I felt in my soul landed softly on the sandy bottom. The silence gathered around me, and the sirens from the town fell away into nothing.

As I lay on the sand, the faint sun drying my skin, a seagull circled twice above my head and then flew away. The wind gently kissed my cheeks. I covered my legs with the sand, like a human sculpture, a mere decoration, an oyster seeking refuge in the sand, anything but a woman of flesh and bone.

CHAPTER THIRTEEN

The next day I slept till late. I opened my windows and inhaled the fresh air. I looked at my calendar and the circled dates of the workshops. My heart squeezed and I pressed my finger against my lips, then I grabbed the calendar page and tore it off.

Tears ran down my cheeks, soon turning into a waterfall, thinking of Gustavo.

The ghosts of my past had followed me. I closed the windows and the curtains.

In the dark room I lay praying for the end of the day. A flicker of sunray crept in happily through the small gap between the curtains. I tried to fall asleep, but the faint sun did not let me. I wrapped my head in a shawl, so as not to see.

I asked myself, weeping: Why does my existence hurt so much?

I wanted my little voice to speak to me. I listened hard, but there was nothing. The walls were deaf and did not hear me calling out for God. My thoughts muffled the cries of my heart. I was drowning in total silence.

Who am I, lying here at the edge of my huge bed?

I did not remember falling asleep. When I opened my eyes, the darkness enveloped me, absorbing my body and my soul. A faint music in the distance penetrated my ears. I tapped my fingers to its rhythm on the night table.

I put on the new dress I bought from my money from my workshops and headed towards the beach. A few people strolled along the sand watching the playful lapping of the waves. I saw a lady collecting shells. I knelt down and picked a shell up too. I pressed the shell against my ear. A murmur of the sea sounded, followed by the melody of lost lovers songs and mermaid legends. All of these sounded in my ear in an instant, all locked in a tiny shell which had once been a home to a tiny creature.

Home? What *is* home? When a tiny creature had once found shelter in this little shell, why is it I feel such an outcast in my own shell, my own body, my own skin, my heart, my soul?

Keep burying yourself alive or abandon yourself to the joy of life. The choice is yours. But remember, you are my choice too. I chose you.

I want to play, I want to try, I want to be alive.

Then go, the world is waiting for you.

I looked up and up and saw the huge golden body of the sun spilling its love, without fear or want, across the canvas of the wide-open sky. I watched my shadow in the sand, it was huge, dark, and beautiful.

'This is me,' I murmured softly. 'This is me.'

It is true, but you are so much more than your shadow.

I strolled along the huge shore and saw the Seagull Boy running towards me, stretching his arms out wide.

'There you are!' he said, grinning.

'Seagull Boy! What a wonderful surprise! So lovely to see you.'

'It is so good to see you as well, Christina.'

He grinned once again.

'Where is your bread?' I said, smiling.

'This time no bread. Just some crumbs for the seagulls.'

He took out a small bag. The seagulls started their dance in the air. The boy opened the bag and scattered the breadcrumbs over the sand. The acrobatics of the seagulls in the air, their shrieking and the whiteness of their feathers filled my eyes with wonder.

'And how are *you*?' the boy asked, once the seagulls had taken up all the breadcrumbs and departed.

'I am not good,' I said.

'And what is the reason for that?'

I dropped my head. Before I could open my mouth to reply, he said: 'Is it about the guy who keeps looking for you and is asking every passer-by if they have seen you?'

'The what? Who? I have no idea who you are talking about.'

'There is a guy in the artist's market asking people if they have seen an artist called Christina.'

I thought of Martin, and tears came to my eyes.

'He said he attended your workshops, and since the shop, where you run these workshops, is ruined he didn't know where else to look for you.'

I wiped my eyes, thinking of poor Gustavo.

'Did he make you sad?' the boy said, softly.

But my heart was too full of pain to speak of that.

'The man,' I asked, 'did he say anything else?'

'But you did not answer my question. Are you sad because of this man? Did he do anything to you? I mean, anything bad?'

'No, darling,' I said. 'He is just a friend of mine. I am worried about the owner of the souvenir shop.'

'I will try to ask my nanny if she knows how he is. Nanny knows everything.'

'Thank you,' I said.

And we stood in silence, our eyes to the sky.

'Look at the seagulls, they know better,' the boy said excitedly. 'There are two flying above our heads. That is not too bad.'

'What do you mean?' I asked.

'Do you believe in superstitions?'

'I do not know,' I said. 'Maybe.'

'Three seagulls is a bad omen. The death of someone. This is what my grandpa used to tell me. And one day it came true, what he said about the three seagulls.'

His face had become so sad. I put my arms around him, and pulled him tight towards me.

'You are such a good boy,' I said. 'Now you go. It is after sunset. Your nanny must be worried.'

I saw his tiny figure disappear slowly into the distance, and I caught a deep breath and made my way home.

CHAPTER FOURTEEN

I went to the market next day, bringing my paintings with me, and set up in my usual spot. As I was displaying them on my stall, a man, probably in his late fifties, stood casting his eyes over them. His hair was dark and reached his shoulders. He was of medium height and wore a burgundy jacket and striped brown trousers. He had a dog on a lead and in the other hand he carried a shopping bag.

'How much are these, madam?' he said. 'I can't see properly. The price on the ticket? My eyes, you know.'

'It depends which,' I said. 'The paintings vary from five to thirty-five euro.'

'Thank you,' he said.

The man paused for a while, as if in thought, and then said: 'Excuse me, madam.' He then went to the side of my stall and began to count the money in his wallet.

He came back round and stood before me.

'Pack all of them for me,' he said. 'I will take them all.'

'All of them?' I said.

I looked at him in disbelief.

'Yes,' he said, smiling, 'All of them.'

I wrapped my paintings in paper and handed them to him, and he handed me all the money in his wallet.

'This should cover it,' he said.

It was too much, but the man refused to pay less.

I couldn't believe my luck. I sold three paintings in two months and now five all in one go. I decided to stay in the market to paint more in case one day the man returned.

When I finished my painting for the afternoon, I looked for Martin. He was not there. I followed the delicious smell of bread to the stall where the Seagull Boy worked instead, but he was not there either. A woman stood behind the stall where the Seagull Boy had once been.

I came closer. It was Sofía.

'Hello, my darling, how are you?' she said.

I asked Sofía where the Seagull Boy was. 'He normally sells his bread here,' I added, 'or maybe I have confused his stall with yours?'

'No, no, it is the same stall. You must be looking for Alejandro.'

'I don't know who that is. I am looking, well...'

I realized right then I didn't even know the real name of the Seagull Boy.

'I am looking for the Seagull Boy.'

She laughed wholeheartedly: 'Then you must be looking for my Alejandro.'

The name Alejandro sounded so distant and unfamiliar to me.

'Oh, this little mischievous boy of mine. He keeps telling people to call him anything but Alejandro.'

The lady sighed and burst into laughter.

'So the Seagull Boy is Alejandro?' I said.

'Yes, he just pretends he doesn't have a real name.'

I smiled to myself, remembering his little speech about names being labels.

'Can I take two loaves of bread, please? They smell incredible.'

Sofía packed two beautifully baked loaves with a crispy crust into a paper bag. Then she added two small rolls with raisins.

'These rolls are a little present from me,' she said, and handed me a small pot with a home-made goat butter. 'They are delicious with this butter.'

'Thank you so much,' I said.

'Just take it as a symbol of my gratitude.'

'Gratitude?' I said opening my eye wide.

'Yes, gratitude. You are a marvellous person. My grandson always tells me about you, how nice and how beautiful you are.'

'I didn't know I meant so much to him.'

Tears filled up Sofía's eyes.

'He adores you,' she said.

'You are the spitting image of my daughter, Alejandro's mum.'

I reached her hand and gave it a gentle squeeze.

'She had beautiful dark blonde hair and such a charming smile – exactly like you. Her eyes reflected the beautiful sea, like yours, and her nose was a bit turned up, again like yours.' She giggled now and gave my elbow a nudge. 'She had many suitors when she was in her twenties,' she added. 'I guess you are the same.'

I blushed. 'I am not in my twenties,' I said.

The lady blushed a little herself, and laughed.

'There is one man who has asked every single seller in the market about you.'

'I know, the Seagull Boy, I mean, Alejandro, told me that he was looking for me. He is a friend of mine.'

I blushed again.

'A friend? If you had seen these man's eyes, how desperately he asked about you, you wouldn't think he is just a friend. His eyes were so full of love.'

'Well, don't friends love each other?' I murmured.

'They do,' the bread lady replied, 'but not in this way, not the way the man looked for you, and asked about you.'

I tried to change the subject. 'Gustavo. He is a good-hearted person. I would really love to find out how he is.'

'Oh, the owner of the souvenir shop?'

I nodded.

The lady hesitated, as if not knowing what to say.

'Please tell me,' I implored.

'He was in hospital for two days,' she said.

'Two days?'

'Yes. The shock from the robbery put him in a bad way for a while.'

'Oh, no. Bless him. Can I see him?'

'I will scribble his address on a piece of paper. I am sure he will appreciate seeing you. Especially as he has no family.'

'I will definitely visit him.'

'Yesterday I cooked a fish soup and Alejandro went on his bike and took it to him,' Sofía said.

'He is such a good boy, Alejandro.'

'Oh yes he is, he is.'

Sofía nodded and smiled, and handed me a piece of paper with Gustavo's address on.

'Thank you,' I said, 'for the address and for the bread.'

'You are most welcome, my darling.'

Sofía waved goodbye, and I left the market.

CHAPTER FIFTEEN

The steep burgundy roof of Gustavo's house had a huge gap on one side in which a thick layer of hay was lodged to prevent the rain coming through. Two big windows at the front faced a beautifully sleepy cherry orchard.

The front door was ajar. A cat peered inside as if waiting for something, impatiently wagging its tail. I pushed the door, and entered the wide hallway. On one side of the hallway a line of family portraits hung lazily and on the other a myriad of potted flowers sat on two narrow shelves. A sweet wave of floral scent filled my nostrils. As I breathed in the sweet aroma, the weakened voice of the elderly shop owner came from somewhere deeper within the house.

'Is anybody there?' he asked.

'It is me,' I called out, walking quickly down the hallway. 'Christina.'

I entered the room where the voice had come from.

'Is it you Tina, my Tina?'

'Yes, it is me.'

'Come in.'

Once I entered the room I saw Gustavo lying motionless on a bed, his face pale, his eyes staring blank at the ceiling.

He turned his eyes to me, and his face beamed. He signalled with his hand to come closer.

'I am a bag of old bones, Christina,' he groaned.

I looked at his eyes and my soul felt an excruciating pain.

'What did they do to you?' I said.

'All my life I put my heart and soul into this beautiful souvenir shop, just to see it in ruins at the end of my life.'

Tears filled his eyes.

My own tears ran wildly down my face.

'I am so sorry,' I said. 'Did they steal a lot?'

'They took my computer, all the money from the till and a lot of stuff from the shop. But what hurts most, my Tina, is the total mess they left the place in. The windows they shattered into pieces, and they smashed everything they did not want to take with them. It is as if they broke into my soul.'

He shut his eyes.

'We will help you to refurbish it,' I said, and held his hand in mine.

Gustavo looked at me.

'You are so sweet, so kind. Bless you,' he said. 'How did you find me?' he asked.

'Sofía gave me your address,' I said.

'Sofía!'

'The bread lady. She is a lovely woman. Have you met Alejandro, her grandson?'

The old man chuckled to himself.

'The boy keeps visiting me and telling me stories. He is amazing. I wish I had a grandson like him.'

'And I wish I had a son like him.'

I blushed, realizing what I had just said. 'I mean, he is a lovely child.'

'His stories, they make me feel much better,' Gustavo said.

'I am glad to hear that,' I said.

'And you, Christina, you have added so much more meaning to my life too.'

'Have I?' I asked. 'I thought I had been more of a burden. You kept helping me. And I have nothing to pay you off for your kindness.'

'You were never a burden, Tina,' he looked fondly into my eyes. 'You have taught me so many things.'

'Like what?' I asked.

'I had lost touch with what it is to feel, investing all my time and money in the business, thinking only about my little shop. I had no time for anyone. And then I saw you. Once I saw you, I knew I had to help.'

'Thank you so much,' I whispered, and tears trickled down my cheeks.

'But, my dear, this is not all that you taught me.'

'No?' I asked, confused.

'No, there are so many beautiful treasures that you carry in your heart, none more important than passion, your hands, with this passion, they create incredible things, all of this comes from your pure golden heart,' he said.

I bowed to him.

'You inspire me, Christina,' he whispered.

'What do you mean?' I asked.

'You know what you want, you will not sacrifice your dreams, you will not compromise, even if it means touching the bottom. Not like me. I am a coward.'

His voice broke down.

He buried his face in his hands.

I placed my hand gently on the top of his head, and said quietly: 'There is no need to call yourself a coward. You are so strong. In spite of everything you managed to achieve something in your life.'

Gustavo took his hands from his face and looked up into my eyes, and spoke.

'Yes, I did. Material things. But material things are not everything. I am old now, and I am just beginning to learn how the world sings so beautifully, how each morning opens my eyes to something new. This opening of my eyes is thanks to you and Alejandro.'

He took a sip of water from a glass by his side, and carried on: 'I was a painter like you once, but I listened to what other people said. They laughed at me when I told them of the idea I had of setting up an association of painters to teach the world to paint. They said I would be better off investing my money in a property like a shop, rather than helping people. I was young, impatient. I wanted quick results, an easier life and money in my pocket. I gave up painting for good. For forty-five years no one ever encouraged me to resume, until you appeared in my life.'

He cleared the tears from his throat, and took another sip of water.

'I didn't know you were a painter,' I said. 'I saw some paint and brushes tucked away on a shelf in the shop, but thought nothing of it. I had no idea that–'

'Yes, they are mine,' Gustavo cut in. 'I haven't used them for years. I guess I am out of practice now.'

'What was once engraved in the heart cannot disappear. It is just a matter of tuning yourself into the beautiful melody of your heart,' I said.

'What if I cannot hear it? What if my heart is dead?' he whispered.

'It is not dead. It sparkles in your eyes,' I said softly, reaching for his hand.

A faint smile appeared on his lips, and he closed his eyes.

'What would I do without you?' he said, almost to himself.

'Rest now,' I said. 'Sleep.'

'You are right.' His voice was weak, and his breath was shallow.

I whispered goodbye and watched him drift away into the land of his dreams.

Outside the sweet aroma of flowers embraced me again, differently this time. I felt as if there was a garden full of flowers growing at the bottom of my heart. I observed how regular my breath was. Just like an ocean wave, coming and going, like the days of my life, marvelling at the love and kindness of people, and at the seagulls dancing beautifully in the air.

CHAPTER SIXTEEN

On my way home from Gustavo's house, I met Alejandro.

I smiled and said: 'Hello Alejandro!'

He looked at me like a wounded dog.

'Who *is* this Alejandro? Did you make a new friend?' he said.

'Your nanny told me–'

'You are right,' he said, still scowling. 'I am Alejandro. But I do not like to use my name.'

'It is such a beautiful name,' I said.

'Yes, I know.' He breathed the air in, deeply and slowly. 'It is just...' he hesitated for a while and then blurted out. 'Names are a nonsense! I have told you I don't like labelling! I am not a label!'

I smiled.

'Maybe you are right, you are a clever boy. And I suspect your reason not to use your name is bigger than one might think.'

He nodded, and then with his finger he pointed at the sky.

'It is dark. It is going to rain,' he said.

I looked up at the gathering clouds. 'Your friends, the seagulls? Do they like the rain?'

'I think they do,' he said, slowly, as if not quite sure, 'if it is just a matter of a few raindrops, but anything more and they seek the shelter of the trees or the cliffs.'

I reflected on what he had just said, and wondered what I would do if I was a seagull.

'I think I am like them,' I said.

'We are all like them,' Alejandro immediately replied. 'We love the sun, the sky, the cliffs, nature, we live in a community, we have babies, we are happy, we are sad, we dance, we cry.'

'Yes, this is so true, the only thing we can't do is fly,' I said with sadness.

'It depends what we understand by flying,' the Seagull Boy stated.

I took my eyes from the heavens, and looked at the face of this small boy. It had some mystery engraved in its features, some lightness, and so much beauty, so much that was hidden.

'These seagulls are majestic,' I said. 'Their life in the air must be extraordinary. Most of us, human beings, we live mundane lives, selling stuff or fishing, going to school or making clothes for people.'

'My grandpa used to say one single seagull can change the way we look at things forever,' he said.

'A single seagull?' I said.

'Yes, just one. Look how they open their wings and reach for the sky,' said the Seagull Boy.

'They are natural flyers,' I said.

'Well, no, actually they are not. Seagulls have to *learn* to fly. They need to be taught – or they will never know. Like us,' he added.

'I do not understand,' I said.

'They do not teach us to fly in school. But my grandpa, he taught me,' the boy said, and looked at me with a strange look upon his face. '*Reach for the sky,* my grandpa would say to me, *dream big in everything you do, then you will fly.*'

My heart filled with love at these words.

'Oh, that is beautiful,' I said. 'I know what you mean now. Your grandpa must have been an incredibly sensitive and beautiful person.'

'He still is,' he said, smiling, spreading his arms out wide as if his grandpa was all around us.

I looked around to see what he meant.

'Está presente, allá arriba y en cada rincón del universo,' the boy said. 'He is everywhere, scattered around like seagull feathers.'

I sighed.

'I have never met such a child like you,' I said.

He shrugged. 'Children are children,' he said. 'We are all the same.'

The Seagull Boy gave me a wink.

'I must hurry now,' he said. 'I am bringing supper to señor Gustavo from the shop. He must be hungry. See you soon, Christina.'

'See you soon.'

And I waved goodbye to the most wonderful boy I had ever met.

I watched his tiny figure disappearing along the beach, as if he had all the time in the world.

'Christina!' he called to me, not even turning his head. 'Never forget about the wings! Never!'

'I won't! I promise!'

I stood motionless, and looked up at the sky from where gentle raindrops began to fall.

First, they landed softly on my hair, then on my cheeks.

Then I felt them everywhere, and before long I was soaking wet.

Open your wings, Christina... and your soul will fly...

CHAPTER SEVENTEEN

The branches of the tree adorned with pink flowers and rustling leaves made a beautiful shelter for me in my little corner of the marketplace, although my feet swam in a big river of the rain as I took my shoes off. I cursed myself for having worn them in the first place.

A familiar voice sounded behind me.

'Such a beautiful lady, her bare feet drowning in the rain.'

I turned and saw Martin.

'Hello,' he said. 'I have found you, at last.'

His eyes pierced mine.

I gave him a faint smile.

'I am missing your workshops,' he said, then cleared his throat and fiddled with the collar of his shirt.

He cleared his throat again.

'And I have missed you,' he said.

I opened my mouth to speak. He reached forward and placed a finger on my lips.

'Please, Christina. Do not worry about me. I know we are friends. Please, let it remain that way. Good friends miss each other, don't they?' A big smile appeared on his face.

I felt my mouth form a smile and my heart skipped a beat.

'Actually,' I said, biting my lower lip, 'I wanted to see you, Martin. I need your help.'

'Always,' Martin replied, his face a picture of concern.

'It is not actually about me,' I said, my voice hesitant and strange.

'That does not matter. Whatever you ask for, I will seek to do. Let us go somewhere first, somewhere dry, and maybe have a little something to eat?' he said.

It was still raining and I was famished.

I lifted my long skirt, and we set off for a nearby café.

'Dinner is on me, Christina,' Martin said, as he pulled a chair out for me to sit.

He took a seat opposite me, and gave me such a warm look, 'Why do you blush so, Christina? We are just two friends together, having a little something to eat.'

'I think this is right for me,' I said, fixing my gaze on the menu, 'vegetable salad with olive bread.'

'How about a piece of good cheese?' he said.

'If you say so,' I said.

When the waiter appeared, Martin took control.

'Could we have,' he said, 'two vegetable salads with olive bread, please, and a large portion of cheese to share?'

Martin then laughed – presumably at the thought of the two of us sharing a large piece of cheese. There was a magical quality to his laugh. I wanted to laugh as well, but the waiter returned with our napkins and our cutlery. I thanked him as he laid them out on the table before us, and left.

'So, what is it?' Martin said in a low tone. 'You said you needed my help. Please do not hesitate to ask me for anything.'

I took a deep breath.

'It is about Gustavo and his shop,' I said.

'How is he? I haven't had any news since the robbery. He must be devastated.'

'He will be okay. He needs to take things easy now. I was wondering if we could help him a bit.'

I looked into Martin's eyes, and I felt so shy.

'Of course,' Martin said. 'What have you in mind?'

'I was thinking of giving him a hand refurbishing the shop. He cannot do it alone.'

'That is a great idea,' Martin said. 'I have a friend also who could help.'

The waiter came with two big plates of salad garnished richly with beautiful leaves of coriander, a huge piece of cheese and a basket of fresh olive bread with crusty skin. We both thanked the waiter, and he left, for another table.

Martin divided the cheese into smaller pieces and put some on my plate.

'Here you are, Christina. ¡Que te aproveche!'

The corners of his eyes raised, and I saw a smile in them.

'Thank you so much,' I said, grabbing the large piece of bread, realizing I knew a little about this man I'd just asked to help me. 'What do you do Martin, for a job?'

'I run a shelter,' he said.

'That sounds interesting,' I said. 'What sort of shelter do you run?'

A glowing light instantly radiated throughout the whole of his face.

'I run a shelter for the displaced and the broken, for the lost and the wounded, uprooted from their environment.'

I looked at him in confusion and wonder.

'Animals,' he added after a while, grinning like a small boy. 'I think I told you before.'

I smiled too. Could this man be any more perfect?

'That sounds amazing,' I said.

'It is a calling. Your true calling will always make your life more interesting, will it not? And, anyway, aren't you doing the same, my dear Christina?'

I blushed.

'I am trying,' I said.

'You are a woman of stamina, Christina. You went through plenty of obstacles to get what you want. This is what I like about you.'

I felt the warm of his breath on my face.

'Still, there is no end to it, these obstacles – what with the shop as it is. But I am supporting my artistic ambitions the best I can.'

I sighed deeply.

Well, I added, 'they are more than just mere ambitions.'

'Tell me more,' Martin said, leaning forward, his elbows resting on the table, his hands embracing each side of his face.

'To be honest,' I said, 'they are my life.'

Martin sat back in his seat, his voice becoming clear and hard and definite.

'Passion sets everything in motion, Christina. It is a life force. We cannot deny it access to our soul. I learnt that from you.'

'There was time not so long ago when I fought against it entering my soul, Martin.'

A tear trickled down my cheek.

'Are you okay, my dear Christina?'

Martin's voice was soft and low and caring. He offered his hand and wiped my face with his fingers.

'Please, do not worry, Martin. It is just... ' I took a deep breath. 'I remember those days when the light in my soul had been switched off. I was so scared of stopping the things that made me so unhappy, so scared of embracing the new.' I gave Martin a faint smile and continued, 'Total darkness surrounded me, until one day I decided that it could not go on.'

'You are such a brave lady, Christina,' Martin said.

'I am not sure if I can call it bravery, Martin. Life pushed me to follow my heart and to quit the things that did not serve me anymore. The side of me that was forever scared died that day, to be reborn the next in the pure glowing light of the rising sun.'

I looked at Martin's face.

'What a beautiful tale,' he said. 'You, Christina, you are like the rising sun. Such a fresh beautiful energy flows from you. I can feel it in your paintings.'

'It is my soul that moves my brush, my hands are a mere tool.'

'That is why your paintings speak in the language of your soul, my dear Christina. I can feel it.'

I felt the melody of his words in my heart, my body quivered and drowned in the warmth.

'Thank you, Martin. I am so grateful I made an acquaintance of you,' I said in a soft voice.

'It is my pleasure also, Christina,' he smiled. 'So where do we begin with helping Gustavo?'

'Let us visit him together tomorrow, Martin. What do you think?'

'That is a good idea.'

'Is the afternoon okay for you? How about meeting about five, by the pier?'

'I will be there,' he said.

'Thank you for today, Christina. I am so glad we managed to meet once more.'

CHAPTER EIGHTEEN

The late afternoon sun gradually sank from the sky, its redness spilling onto the vast waters below, waves dancing madly, sending foam splashing and bouncing in the cool breeze. My eyes joined in this dance, registering every detail of the scene in all four corners of my soul. I indulged in the warmth of the fading sun and stretched my arms out wide, and felt a warm breath on the back of my neck.

'My dear Christina, how are you?'

I turned quickly.

'Hello, Martin.'

The glow of the sun reflected on our faces.

'You are so beautiful in the fading sun,' Martin said, and I blushed.

'Shall we go now?' I asked.

'Do you mind if we stay for a while, Christina? It is so beautiful here.'

We watched the sky till the last glow of the sun disappeared from the horizon.

'We should go now,' I said, 'we must not keep Gustavo up late.'

Martin stopped at the end of the pier and gave me his hand on the stairs. 'Please,' he said, and smiled so beautifully.

'Thank you,' I said, my breath coming in short bursts as I walked down the stairs leading to the beach.

As my feet landed on the moist sand, I removed my shoes and walked barefoot, while Martin cast a wistful glance at the ferries in the distance.

'Once, you know, Christina,' he said, 'I wanted to work at sea.'

'Really?' I raised my eyebrows. 'When was that?' I asked.

'I was a little boy in South America. My dad said that if it was something I really wanted, it would happen.'

'But it didn't?'

'No, Christina, it did not. Certain dreams are short-lived, I suppose. They were simply the dreams of a little boy. When I grew up, I realized it really was just a dream.'

'I thought all dreams were a calling of the soul.'

'They are, Christina. I believe that too. But sometimes, they are to help us realize what we do not want,' said Martin.

'How is it possible?'

I frowned at him.

'It is very simple, my dear. You see, some dreams come from the bottom of our hearts – they are our calling. Like you said about the calling of our souls. Once you achieve those dreams, you know you have found what you want in this world. And…' he hesitated for a while, as if reflecting on what he had just said.

'How about other dreams, aren't they real?' I asked, looking closely at his serious face.

'The other dreams, it is not that they are not real. They come from our ego. You can achieve them, but once you do so, you are no longer interested in having achieved them.'

'What do you mean?' I asked.

'You know it is not something that makes you happy. You thought you wanted it because your ego, attached so strongly to society and its opinions, pushed you to do so.'

I stopped.

'What is it?' he asked, shyly. 'Are you okay, Christina?'

'You just made me think about what I used to do for my living,' I said.

'And what was that?' he asked.

'I was a nurse.'

'I had no idea. I thought you had always been a painter, or at least an art teacher, or something.'

'It was my dream to study fine arts at the university when I reached the age of eighteen, but I did not manage to realize it.'

'What happened? Why did you not realize your dream?' he asked.

'I was a coward, Martin. I listened to the opinions of other people, that being a nurse is a respectable job and I would be better off working in a hospital than spending my life hanging around artists in exhibition halls earning a pittance.'

I could taste the bitterness on my tongue.

'People!' Martin said, shaking his head. 'People and their *opinions*!'

'Don't get me wrong, Martin, I really like helping people, but the pressure of the job was too much for me.' Tears appeared in my eyes. 'To watch so many people dying was unbearable.'

'I am sure you were a fantastic nurse,' Martin said, softly, pulling me close to him as we continued along the path to Gustavo's house.

And for the rest of the way, we walked in silence.

The tree branches near the house swayed gently in the wind and the rustle of leaves filled the air with a beautiful melody. A fat, stripy cat lay on the doormat, seemingly oblivious to the smallest noise around him.

I came up to the spacious window and gazed within. The furniture inside the living room loomed silently out of the darkness. As my eyes adjusted to the darkness, I saw an indistinct figure bending over Gustavo.

'Come, Martin!' I called. 'Gustavo seems to have a guest.'

'Really? At this time?' Martin said.

I knocked on the door.

An eerie silence filled the air around us. The trees stood still now, even the bluebells in the garden stopped shaking their beautiful heads for a moment. Only the cat woke up, stretched his paws slowly, then his whole body and walked imperiously away. I do not know how long we stood there, my heartbeat accelerating with every darkening second.

I knocked on the door again.

A lady finally opened the door. Two black irises floated in the vast blueness of her eyes, carrying me away as if on the waves of the sea.

'How can I help you?' she said, a faint smile moving the deep-set wrinkles around her eyes and her mouth. I looked straight into her sapphire blue eyes, and found myself floating, floating, floating.

Gustavo's voice sounded through the thick walls.

'Is that you, Christina? My lovely Christina, is that you?'

The lady opened the door wider, and I followed Martin into the house.

'Yes, it is me,' I answered.

As I entered the living-room, I found Gustavo seated in a big armchair.

'What a surprise!' I said.

'I feel better, that's why I thought it is good to sit in this armchair, rather than lie in the bed.'

'That's a good idea,' Martin said.

'Please, meet Ines, my neighbour. Ines and her husband are so nice and always come to help me.'

Gustavo pointed at Ines, the lady who had let us in.

Ines took my hands warmly in hers.

'It is a pleasure to meet you, my dear,' she said. 'I have heard so much about you.'

She smiled and her sapphire eyes twinkled.

'It is a pleasure to meet you too,' I said, and introduced Martin to Ines.

'I know this lad,' Gustavo said, peering at Martin, 'he came to your workshop, don't you remember, Christina?'

'Yes,' I said, smiling. 'I remember.'

'I am old, but I still have a good memory, Christina,' and Gustavo laughed with all his heart before breaking into a fit of coughing.

'I must go now, Gustavo,' Ines said, and bowed so gracefully to us. 'If you need me, just let me know.'

'Thank you, Ines. What would I do without you?' Gustavo replied, tears forming in his eyes.

As Ines bowed gracefully to us as she left, those sapphire eyes of hers were wet with tears.

The old man composed himself once more, and a brighter colour came to his face.

'Martin... Christina...' he said, with a big smile, 'please, sit. It is so nice to see you together.'

Martin and I sat each on the sofa, facing Gustavo.

'My lovely Tina,' he said. 'I am so glad you are here.'

Martin looked at me and I felt my cheeks burn.

'I... I mean... we... we came with a suggestion. An offer of assistance,' I said.

Gustavo sat up, a little surprised.

'We want to help you renovate your shop,' Martin said. 'After the robbery, it does not look good.'

'Renovate?' Gustavo said.

His face grew pale.

'Yes, is there anything wrong with that?' I asked.

'No, no,' he looked at us. 'It is just I... I... just sold it.'

'No, you cannot...'

My lips quivered.

'Dear Christina, I had no idea you liked it so much. I...' and Gustavo's voice broke and he burst into tears.

Martin held my hand and then turned to Gustavo.

'Please, please,' he said. 'Let us talk about it. Maybe it is not too late...'

'It is done, Martin. But thank you. And Christina, do not worry. You will still have your workshops. I have a plan.'

The old man wiped his tears from his face.

'It is not about the workshops,' I said. This time it was the turn of my voice to break. 'I love that shop. It meant so much to me. I...'

Martin held my shaking hands in his.

'I simply do not understand why,' I continued. 'Why did you not tell me about it? I thought we were friends.'

Gustavo's face creased with pain, his eyes glistening with the hurt he had caused me.

'We *are* friends, my dear. Even more than that. You are like my daughter. I just didn't have the opportunity to tell you. It happened so quickly.'

'Too quickly,' I retorted.

'Christina, please let me explain.'

I felt the anger and the bitterness rising within me.

'What explanation have you got? It is your shop, you have a right to do anything you want with it.'

'Please, my dear Tina. Let me explain. Please.'

I breathed deep, feeling some of the anger leave me as I did so.

'Okay.'

Gustavo told me his shop lost its soul after the robbery and that he thought it was a sign for his life to take a new course.

I nodded while he continued.

'Do you remember our conversation that we had last time about my lost dreams and ideals?'

'Yes,' I murmured, remembering his words, 'but what does the selling the shop have to do with your ideals?'

'It is time to move on,' he said. 'It is time to start a new adventure. It is time to follow my dreams. I sold the shop and I am going to use the money for setting up an association to support young aspiring artists like you, my dear Christina.'

My hand tightened on Martin's.

I couldn't believe my ears.

CHAPTER NINETEEN

After we left Gustavo's house, Martin and I headed back towards the beach. We walked in silence. The moon gazed at us, wondering what was happening in our hearts. I looked up at its pale face, I felt weak, so I sat down on the pebbles.

'Leave me here, Martin,' I said.

'Are you sure?' Martin asked, frowning at me.

'Yes, Martin. I am sure.'

Martin hesitated. 'It is chilly.'

'It does not matter,' I said.

And that is where we stayed there, me sitting on the pebbles and him standing before me, gazing out at the ocean, both of us in silence.

'Is it all about the shop?' he finally said, then hesitated once more, 'or is it… something else?'

'I need peace, that's all. Thank you for always being around. Thank you for everything.'

He turned round to me, at last.

I gave him a faint smile.

'I understand, Christina,' he said. 'You need to rest. I will see you tomorrow.'

'Goodbye, Martin.'

Sat by myself in the light of the moon, the waves crashing against the shore, I sighed heavily and curled up like a cat. I smelt the freshness of the sea, the cool night breeze tickling my nostrils. I covered myself with my shawl and fell asleep under the starry sky.

I dreamt about the moon that night. It wondered where my lover was. I had met him half-way and rejected him. Like a wounded wolf he marched away. I entered the dark channel. It was cold inside and the humidity irritated my throat.

I felt nauseous. A mysterious woman grabbed my hand. She was dressed in white robes and kept smiling at me. I knew I had met the Goddess in my heart, and I fell in love with her. Nothing else mattered anymore. I felt the warmth of her light on my cheeks melt my icy heart. My body relaxed.

I was at peace.

Half-awake and half-asleep, my cheeks pressed against the sand, I awoke the following morning to the sound of shrieking seagulls. My palms were moist and warm yet my body shivered and ached. I sat up and stretched to ease the pain, and saw a bunch of beautiful roses next to me. I reached over to smell them. They were, indeed, beautiful.

In the distance I saw the young man carrying a huge basket of crimson roses. He was singing, *Rosas, rosas para los enamorados. Rosas para las mujeres y rosas para los hombres.*

His words appeared as a little chant echoing in my heart. *Rosas, rosas* sang my heart, *Rosas, hay rosas en mi alma...*

I stretched on the sand and yawned, and was ready to head towards my cottage, when I noticed Alejandro kneeling before me. His face was buried in his hands.

'Seagull Boy!' I said joyfully. 'How nice to see you!'

Alejandro lowered his hands, and looked at me, his face swimming in a river of tears.

I wrapped my arms around his shoulders

'What is it my dear?' I said. 'What is it?'

'My nanny,' he said. 'She does not understand.'

'Understand what?' I asked.

He broke into loud sobs.

'Does it matter?' he said, looking up at me, tears of pain replaced with tears of fury. 'Who cares in this world? If only my grandpa was alive. And my mum.'

He sighed heavily and covered his face with his hands again.

'Oh please, my dear, my baby.'

I drew his quivering body into my arms. His body fell into them willingly. I felt the heart beating in his tiny body. I don't know for how long we sat like that – the Seagull Boy and I.

We merged with the sea and the sun and the sky — a single spiritual being, floating. We were like seagulls.

My chest was so light and I saw a rainbow smile stretch across the sky.

Everything whispered: *love, love, love.*

The boy's voice brought me back from my reverie. 'You are so nice,' he said. His muffled voice echoed through my body.

'I love you so much,' I whispered, and I felt the warm wave of his love embrace my body.

'You are like my mama,' he said.

I hugged him even tighter.

'So tell me, Seagull Boy, what is up? What does your nanny not understand?'

He released himself from my arms gently and his face grew sullen again.

'She understands nothing,' he mumbled.

'What do you mean understands nothing?' I said in a soft voice. 'I think you need to tell me what happened.'

'My teacher came to my nanny and was furious. She told her that I miss school very often and I need to...' He stopped and took a deep breath, '*rectify* this situation. I don't even know what *rectify* means.'

The poor boy. So wise, yet so much to learn.

'The teacher meant that you need to go to school regularly,' I said very gently, trying not to upset him more.

'School is nonsense!' he snarled.

I had not the courage to say any more.

'Don't tell me you agree with her!' he yelled, jumping to his feet and standing before me, his fists tightly clenched.

'I am angry! I am angry!' His cheeks grew like the two balloons, as he stomped his feet on the sand.

My eyes shed tears, it was that funny, and the laughter burst out of me.

'You think it is funny? I will run away! I will run away!'

'Look at the seagulls,' I said, 'they must be laughing too.'

The Seagull Boy looked at the sky, his mouth wide open, and the anger slowly drained out of him.

'I am sorry, Christina. For shouting. It's just–'

I pulled him back to me and wrapped him in my arms.

'I know,' I said. 'I know.'

When the Seagull Boy left, I sat alone on the beach listening to the waves beating against the shore. My heart tuned into the rhythm – the coming and the going.

There are certain people that leave our lives, but soon new people come and fill our hearts with joy. My body glowed in the sun as if my very soul was aflame.

And I longed to see Gustavo.

CHAPTER TWENTY

I found Gustavo outside the house sitting in the shade. His eyes gazed at the ground and his hands rested on his knees.

'Good morning,' I said.

'Dear Christina, my Tina,' he said, his face beaming. 'How nice to see you! Please, sit.'

A small crack came from the chair as Gustavo attempted to stand.

'I am so happy to see you as well,' I said. 'But please sit,' I said, taking a place on the chair beside him. 'You need your rest. I came to apologise. I should not have acted like I did when you told me about the shop. I am sorry.'

He sighed heavily and held my hands in his.

'I should have told you before, Tina, but everything happened so quickly. You were not around and–'

'Please, do not worry. I was a bit overwhelmed yesterday when you told me, but I am fine now.'

'Soon, my dear, you will have your place for your workshops. Just trust me.'

He winked at me, his eyes sparkling as I had never seen them before.

'My first job is to pass on to people what I always had in my heart, and let it grow in theirs.'

'And what is that?' I asked.

'This passion for life. The passion for life I rediscovered, thanks to you, dear Christina.'

He smiled and I smiled too.

'People may say I've lost my mind,' he said, 'but I do not care.'

'Let them say what they want,' I said.

With such bliss in my heart I stretched my arms towards the sun, letting it caress my cheeks gently. The sunrays were like the arms of the lover I longed for. I let them kiss my lips and I let my body bathe in the golden river flowing from the sky.

The voice of Gustavo brought me back down to earth.

'Come to me at the end of the week,' he said, 'I will have more information about this beautiful project then.'

'I will do that,' I said, and gave him a light kiss on his brow.

I fell asleep very early that day. My cottage was so very small, but so very cosy. The dark clouds of the past no longer hung above me in eerie silence. That night I awoke and painted a picture of a woman in a ragged dress.

She smiled out of the canvas at me, and I smiled back at her. I saw such a beautiful light in her eyes. My soul felt at home with this woman, as if I had known her all my life. Tears of happiness trickled down my face.

My sweating hands touched the painting and gently stroked the woman's cheek.

CHAPTER TWENTY-ONE

I was walking on the beach, the sand jumping joyfully as I stepped on it, picking up some shells to decorate my stall.

When I arrived at the marketplace, I arranged the shells I'd collected on the old cardboard boxes that constituted my stall, and displayed my paintings. The beach was not far, stretching its golden body and glistening in the sun.

I heard a voice behind me.

¿Cuánto cuesta?' the man said, and pointed at my latest painting.

'I'm sorry,' I said, 'this one is not for sale. It is not finished yet.'

It was the painting of the ragged woman I had begun last night.

'So why did you bring it here?' he asked.

'I wanted to finish it off at the market here today.'

'I tell you it is finished,' the man insisted.

I looked at the painting and tried to see it through his eyes, but I could not and did not want to sell it. The ragged woman in so short a time had become a part of me. I could not bear to let her go. But then again, I needed the money.

'If you think it is finished, you can have it for ten euros,' I said.

I handed him the painting.

'For this, I will pay you at least three times as much. It is a real masterpiece.'

I cleared my throat. *Three times as much?* And it isn't even finished? 'It is a very personal painting,' I said.

'It is very personal to me also. Today I have found a piece of myself that has been missing all my life. It has a rawness that speaks to me and tugs at my heart.'

The man handed me thirty-five euros.

'Thank you, sir,' I said, overcome with emotion at his words. Then without much thinking I blurted out, 'Bless you.'

He bowed to me, took my painting and was gone very quickly. I frantically ran my fingers through my old paintings, thinking about how to display them, already missing the unfinished painting of the ragged woman. I placed my hand on my heart, closed my eyes and breathed deep, and heard the little voice coming from the bottom of my heart.

Let the world receive the gift of these fingers which create so effortlessly. Let the world receive the purity of your broken soul which spills onto the canvas. Let the world receive the image of your loving heart.

My pulse accelerated, I knew that a part of me was gone with the selling of the picture of the ragged woman, but the awareness that it was never mine to covet comforted me beyond measure.

That morning I spent a lot of time painting and observing the crowds of people passing through the streets of the market. I had been sitting in this way for a couple of hours when I saw the bent figure of Martin, evidently looking for something – or someone. Our eyes suddenly met. A million thoughts and feelings began to churn inside me, devouring my heart.

Martin made his way through the crowds towards me.

'How are you?' he said. 'It is very crowded here today.'

'And I need space for creating,' I replied, and laughed.

'But look at this mighty sea over there, Christina, it is a huge space – the inspiration for a thousand paintings.'

'I know. But still in my soul I feel I even need more space than that.'

Martin came closer, and leaned down on his haunches before me.

'Is it about me?' he said.

My heart beat faster.

'Nope.'

His eyes looked into mine so deeply and fondly.

'Are you sure, dear Christina?'

And my heart beat faster still.

'You are my great support, Martin, a true friend.'

'So, what is it about your space, Christina?' he replied, standing up once more – towering over me.

'I am scared,' I said.

'Scared of what?'

In truth, the man paying so much for my painting of the ragged woman had really frightened me.

'Of opportunities,' I said.

I forced a smile.

'Opportunities? What do you mean *opportunities*?'

'I was scared when Gustavo told me about selling his shop, and about the new project.'

'It seems he wants you to be a big part of it.'

'Last night I went and apologised to Gustavo about leaving without any word the other day. I felt so sorry for him,' I said.

'You are such a big-hearted person, Christina.'

Martin blushed. He hesitated for a while, and then said,' I love your soul.'

I closed my eyes and let my ears absorb his words, their musicality permeating my heart. I opened my eyes and the whiteness of seagulls floating in the air spread in front of me.

I closed my eyes again and felt his hand on mine.

I realised soon that the noise from the market was petering out, as people started packing away.

'Martin, I need to pack my stuff as well,' I told him.

'I will help you,' he smiled.

We wrapped my paintings in the newspapers. I felt so hungry, I checked if I still had money in my pocket.

Martin pointed to his car.

'I will take you home,' he said.

'I was planning to walk,' I said. 'I need to do some shopping.'

'That's not a problem,' Martin replied. 'I'll stop on the way and you can do your shopping then.'

We put my stuff in the car boot and Martin drove me to the fruit and vegetable market. My eyes examined different types of fruit. I craved them all – the passion fruit, mangoes, papayas, grapes, bananas. I filled my basket and reached into the pocket of my skirt to pay the fruit seller, but Martin grabbed the basket from me and asked the seller how much the basket of fruit would come to.

'Martin, it is really nice of you,' I protested, 'but I do have money on me.'

'It doesn't matter,' Martin said, 'keep it for something else.'

I uttered a simple thank you to him, and we came back to the car. Martin put the shopping in the boot and took me home.

'I forgot to tell you something,' he said, as we walked side by side across the beach to my house.

I looked across at him suspiciously.

'Is it good or bad news?' I said.

'Do you remember your friend Marina you were looking for, Christina?'

'Have you seen her?' I asked.

'No, I heard about her.'

I clapped my hands. 'How is that possible?'

'I bumped into her neighbour and she told me that Marina is on her way from Peru. She had planned to meet you on your arrival in Gran Canaria, but her mother-in-law took ill, and her and her husband flew back to tend to her. Marina's husband will be staying until his mother recovers.'

'Bless her and her family,' I said. 'I am so grateful to count her as my friend. I can't believe I have survived without her.'

'You more than survived, Christina. You are blooming as an artist, and as a woman.'

I noticed how his face turned red on uttering these last words.

'It really has been a journey, Martin,' I said.

'A beautiful journey, Christina.'

Martin's voice sounded so gentle and caring.

I looked up into the sky. The seagulls circled above our heads.

'It is the journey of seagulls,' I whispered, but Martin didn't seem to hear me as he too looked up in wonder at the spectacular dancing birds above his head.

CHAPTER TWENTY-TWO

Martin and I sat outside a café in the town, drinking coffee. I was so excited about the news that Marina was on her way back to Gran Canaria.

'When is she coming?' I asked Martin.

'In a few days,' Martin said.

'My beautiful friend is coming. I miss her so much.'

'Where did you two meet, Christina? Just out of curiosity.'

It all came back to me. That very first day.

'At university,' I said. 'In Glasgow. Marina had received a scholarship and used the opportunity to study abroad.'

I took a sip of coffee.

'Marina and I often took weekend trips away into the country,' I continued, 'wandering through the beautiful mountains of Scotland.'

'When I was a little boy my grandpa used to take me on trips to Glasgow,' Martin murmured. 'It is a splendid city.'

'Oh Scotland,' I said, and sighed heavily. 'It is such a beautiful country.'

'There is a sadness in your voice,' Martin said. 'What is it?'

I blew out a long breath.

'Scotland is where I met my husband. In the hospital in Glasgow where I was doing my placement. Later we moved to London.'

'Your husband?' he said, unable to hide his surprise.

'I mean my *ex*-husband. He is not worth talking about it.'

We sipped our coffee in silence. There was a heaviness between us I could not stand, like the feeling of an approaching storm.

'Martin?'

'Yes, Christina.'

'Have you ever loved a woman?'

Martin looked surprised. 'I did. Once. She is gone now. She has been gone a long time.'

'I do not understand,' I said, and looked at Martin's quivering lips.

'I was a young boy living his dreams. I studied veterinary medicine in the city of my grandparents – Edinburgh. I loved what I was doing, and I dreamt big. Soon after completing my studies, I arrived in Spain. I was very poor, but ambitious. Very soon I got a lucrative post as a vet. I met a girl on the beach on a sunny day. She appeared like mist from heaven. She was as gentle as the sky and as radiant as the morning sun.'

'We began to date, and I quickly fell in love. At first, her mother seemed to accept our relationship. Later, however, when she found out I gave up my job at the clinic to establish a shelter for rescued animals and was studying to be an exotic vet, she got very upset. She told me one day that my passion for these animals would leave nothing for her daughter. I told her I loved her daughter.'

'But at the bottom of my heart I knew it was her way of saying I was not good enough for her daughter. It hurt like a hell to realise that. We broke up soon after, and her daughter married another man. All the stars and birds witnessed and blessed our love. But it was not to be.'

I sighed heavily.

'I promised myself that I would never love again,' Martin said, quietly.

Tears fell like stones from my cheeks.

'What a beautiful story,' I said.

Martin's lips tightened, and he said, 'She got pregnant soon after marrying the guy her mum chose for her, and a little boy was born. When I was coming back home from the shelter one day, her mother stopped me on the road. She told me that she was gone. I couldn't understand what she was saying, at first. Then the look in her eyes told me everything. She managed to utter her daughter's name, and I collapsed to my knees.'

'It was the darkest day I have ever experienced in my life. Even finding out that she married a different man before was not so devastating as the news of her death.'

'Her death?' I couldn't manage to stop my own tears.

'She died in a car crash. Her husband was with her, he also died.'

'What happened to the boy?'

'He was four years old when his parents were killed. His grandma and grandpa brought him up. Then his grandpa died. He lives with his grandma now. He is a good boy. I dared not speak to him, though he has his mother's eyes. We both share a love of animals. He is a little expert on seagulls, you know? They call him the Seagull Boy. You probably know him.'

And the ground slowly began to open up beneath my feet.

CHAPTER TWENTY-THREE

I collapsed on my bed and covered my face with my hands.

How is it possible? *How?* The Seagull Boy, his mum, Sofía, Martin? All of them connected. And what about the Seagull Boy's dad?

I had no idea what time I fell asleep.

I felt the warmth of the sun as it danced on my face in the early morning, and I slowly opened my eyes. I heard a knocking on my door. I sprang to my feet and slipped into my dress.

I ran my shaking fingers through my tangled hair, and made my way to the door.

'Who is there?' I said.

Silence. I pressed my ear against the thick wooden door. A restless breathing filled the silence. And, finally, a voice, sweet and familiar.

'Please, let me in!'

I gazed at the door and froze. I could not speak. With my palm sweating, I yanked the door open.

'Marina!' I exclaimed, and fell into her arms.

She drew me even closer and I could hear her heart beating madly in her tiny body.

'Oh, Christina! My dear friend!'

We stood holding each other for what seemed an eternity, tears tumbling down our cheeks.

Marina eventually drew back and wiped her face, and mine.

'How are you, my dear, dear Christina? How have you been?'

'I expected you to come in a few days,' I said. 'But here you are!'

'I took an earlier flight from Peru,' she said.

'And I'm so glad you did. Come in, come in,' I said.

We sat on the settee, close together, our hands clasped as old friends do.

'Tell me everything, Marina. How is your mum-in-law, and your husband?'

'They are all right now,' Marina said, and squeezed my hands. 'I am so glad you got the key to my summer cottage, Christina.'

'It is a beautiful place,' I said. 'I don't know what I would have done without you, Marina.'

Tears fell from my eyes once more, though they were different tears. Tears of loss and pain.

'What is the matter, Christina? What has happened?'

I told Marina my whole story beginning with my arrival in Spain, then losing my savings, being destitute and ending up sleeping in a park.

'I am so sorry you went through such an ordeal,' Marina said. 'If I had been here…'

'It is all right, Marina, you weren't to know this would happen. Please don't blame yourself.'

I tried to smile through my tears, and gave her a warm hug.

'So, you met Martin, the guy that bought the house from me,' she smiled, wiping away tears of her own. 'He is such a good man,' she added.

My face beamed.

Marina peered at me closely, and grinned.

'It is *not* what you think,' I replied, softly, feeling sure Marina could hear the beating of my heart.

'And what do I think?'

'We are good friends,' I said. 'Nothing more.'

'Don't be so defensive, my dear Christina. Martin is a very handsome man. A very handsome *single* man.'

Marina giggled.

I giggled.

We were like two fifteen-year-old girls, one discovering the other had a crush on a boy in class.

After many hours of catching up, and several coffees, it was time for Marina to return home.

We walked together along the beach under the moonlight, as if we had never been parted. Eventually, we reached a very peaceful neighbourhood with fabulous private houses.

Marina pointed at a magnificent house with a very steep roof and orange wooden shutters. A rose bush climbed the walls, and despite not having roses now, it decorated the house beautifully.

'That is my new house, Christina. I hope you like it.'

I took a deep breath. It was marvellous.

'There are others that may be better around here, Christina, but we wanted to live closer to the beach and the town so, for us, this is perfect.'

As we entered the house, Marina directed me to take a seat in the front room.

'I know that other house at the end of the forest lane,' I called from where I sat. 'Martin lives there. I saw it when I was looking for your cottage.'

'We didn't want to move too far,' Marina said, coming in from the kitchen with a tray of jasmine tea and some biscuits.

'It is such a shame you didn't know that I had moved, Christina. I sent you the message, but it was too late I suppose. Please help yourself to some biscuits,' she added.

I took a sip of the tea, and my mind began to wander.

'Without the goodness of the people that have helped me – Gustavo, Martin, Sofía, her grandson, and you, Marina – I would have nothing.'

'What did I do? I was not even here.'

My mind shot back to my time with Philip.

'Marina, if it hadn't been for your big heart and your friend's invitation to your summer cottage, I do not know what would have become of me when my marriage ended. I love you so much.'

'I love you too, Christina.'

CHAPTER TWENTY-FOUR

I awoke early next morning, still wondering if what had happened yesterday was true – if Marina really was back. She had offered me to stay in her house till her husband returned, but I rejected her offer. I wanted to stand on my own two feet. With the money I earned from tutoring and the sale of my paintings, I could possibly rent a flat in a decent area soon. Life was teaching me to be strong in the face of numerous hardships, and I knew I could manage on my own. From the mists of pain, my mind was becoming as pristine as meadows full of flowers swaying gently in the wind. It was time to meet Gustavo and talk about his project.

I walked towards his house for roughly twenty minutes. The sun was shining, and I stretched my hands to catch its warmth. I paused and smiled at the sky. When I reached the Gustavo's house, he was waiting for me outside.

'There you are, my dear,' Gustavo said with a warm smile. 'I was about to come over to see you. We need to talk about the project.'

He put his arm through mine and led me into the house and through to the garden.

'You will run workshops for inexperienced artists,' he said as we walked. 'You will teach not just the techniques of painting, but the right *attitude* towards painting. You are simply wonderful at that.'

'I need to prepare myself,' I said. 'I need to refresh my knowledge. It is very different – painting for yourself to explaining all this to others.'

Gustavo raised his eyebrows.

'Have you not done something similar with Martin?'

'I have, but that was different. Martin is a friend.'

'A friend?' Two lines formed on Gustavo's forehead.

'Yes. That is why I feel at ease running workshops with him.'

'I thought a guy like him would be more interested in dating you rather than attending your workshops.'

I was unexpectedly angry at Gustavo for speaking this way about Martin.

'He runs an animal shelter and is interested in painting animals,' I said. 'He has no interest in me beyond teaching him to paint.'

I felt my anger rising with each word I spoke.

'And besides,' I said, staring directly into Gustavo's eyes, 'don't you think we are straying a little away from our topic?'

'I am sorry, Christina. Please forgive an old man his fun. Let us focus on the project.'

'Why is everyone pushing me into the arms of a man that I met in such unfavourable circumstances? Do you think he can save me, or something?'

'What do you mean *everyone*, Christina? Who else told you the same thing?'

Gustavo raised his eyebrows.

'It does not matter who. Let us change the subject.'

I felt the burn ease from my cheeks, and a calmness return to my voice.

'As you wish, dear Christina.'

'Thank you,' I said.

'The venue for our workshop,' Gustavo continued, 'will be in the same place as before.'

This time it was my turn to raise my eyebrows.

'But you told me you had sold the shop.'

'Yes, Christina, but not the extension – the studio. This is where you will continue your workshops and have your office.'

'My office?'

'Yes, there will be some admin to deal with, advertising the workshops, organising the competitions.'

'Competitions?'

'This is going to be big, Christina. All the money I have is going into this project, and I am certain we can get funding from other organisations. Maybe even sponsors. You will be paid for everything. I have worked for nearly fifty years for this. We will be an independent organisation – artists helping artists.'

'That is a wonderful idea,' I said.

'All my life I have dreamt about running such an organisation as this.' Tears appeared in his eyes. 'I longed to be an artist myself, but it was not to be.'

He wrapped his arms around mine, and I felt his tears on my cheeks.

'Thank you, Christina, for helping me realise my dream.'

'Me?' I said.

'You are such a brave lady, Christina. You have taught me to follow the true calling of my heart. I always ignored this calling, but watching you follow yours has given me the courage to follow mine.'

'I had always the feeling I caused you nothing but trouble.'

'Christina, never say that! You are as my daughter and I love you like a father!'

I had no words to say.

'Let us meet tomorrow, Christina. I am tired. There is much we still need to discuss.'

I caught a glimpse of the dark blue sky during my evening walk along the beach. The scattered clouds formed strange shapes. A solitary seagull floated tirelessly in the air and shrieked as if in search of his companions.

No creature responded.

Oh, how I wished I could fly, so I could tell him I was coming.

CHAPTER TWENTY-FIVE

The next day, I heard a soft knocking on my door.

'Marina, is that you darling?' I whispered.

'Yes, it is me, please open the door.'

As I opened the door, we hugged, and Marina opened a small box.

'This is for you Christina.'

I smelt something sweet.

'Almond cake! How lovely!'

'I made it especially for you.'

I wondered what had brought Marina so early to my door. She looked very calm, her face radiating with happiness. As we sat there together drinking tea, I thought about how easy her life was. She had a beloved husband and an amazing house with a beautiful garden. And this summer cottage. I looked at the corner of the room where my small wardrobe stood. My stuff didn't even fill the half of it.

'The cake is delicious,' I said, trying to hide the emptiness I felt inside. 'You could sell cakes like this easily at the market, like Sofía sells her bread.'

'It is too time-consuming,' Marina replied. 'Maybe one day. You know Sofía?'

'She is very kind,' I said. 'A beautiful lady.'

Marina put her tea on the table and sat back in her chair, smiling at me mischievously.

'You are getting to know everyone around here, it seems, Christina.'

I forced a smile.

'How about Martin?'

I studied Marina's face, thinking it was so much prettier than my own.

'Martin? We are on good terms,' I said. 'He has helped me so much. I really do appreciate him.'

Marina nodded her head. 'Tell me, my sweet friend,' she said. 'Do you care for him?'

I closed my eyes and felt a smile appear on my face.

'You are my best friend, Marina, so I can tell you. But please do not breathe a word to anyone. I do not just like him. I like him *a lot*. He told me he loves me, but I am not willing to enter a relationship. I want us only to be friends.'

Marina shifted in her seat.

'Be careful, Christina,' she said. 'Men are sensitive. If you do not return his feelings, there may come a time where he may turn his back on you, and he will be gone forever.'

There was such an apprehensive look in her eyes.

'Martin would never do that. I am sure.'

'I hope that you are right my sweet friend. I do hope.'

Marina smiled, and I felt a warm wave of love embrace my heart.

'Life is so short,' she said.

'Thank you, Marina. You are such a good friend.'

'I am always here for you, Christina. Never forget that. Now, what are you up to today?'

'I am going to see Gustavo to plan the refurbishment of his studio for our workshops.'

'Is Martin coming?' she asked.

I was getting a little fed up that Marina kept mentioning Martin.

'Why are you asking?' I said. 'And no, he is not coming.'

I knew Marina wanted to continue talking about Martin, and as she began to speak again, I said: 'Please, Marina. No more.'

'I am sorry, Christina. No more questions about Martin. Honest. But I will go with you to Gustavo's house. I want to lend you my support. I want to be there for you as I was not here when you arrived in Spain.'

I saw the tears in her eyes.

'It is okay, Marina. I will be fine.'

'The least I can do is walk with you to Gustavo's house,' Marina said, standing to go.

'I would love that,' I said.

As we walked along the beach, it was as if all the birds seemed to wake up at once, their sweet loud chirruping filling our ears. I wanted this walk along the beach to last forever, to sink into the beautiful melody of it all. We walked in silence. Marina seemed preoccupied with something, but whatever it might be she kept to herself. When we reached Gustavo's house, he greeted us in a warm manner, and Marina wished us a good day, and left.

'Come in, my dear Christina,' Gustavo said. 'I have some tea with freshly baked biscuits waiting. Alejandro has just brought them.'

My heart leapt in remembrance of the Seagull Boy.

'Is he still here?' I asked. 'Alejandro?'

'No, he left a few minutes ago. He said he was late for school.'

I could not hide my surprise.

'School!'

'Yes, Christina. Little Alejandro is finally going to school.'

We laughed much that day, myself and Gustavo. But it was not all laughing. We chose the colour of the paint for the walls of the studio; we designed a logo for our organisation, and priced up my paintings for an exhibition.

Sitting with Gustavo in his beautiful house, I realised something important, as if a part of myself was slowly fixing itself. *Home* is not a place. We carry our homes within ourselves, and we take them with us wherever we go.

With deep gratitude in my heart, I returned home in the evening along the beach under the cold night sky, and climbed easily into bed. I wrapped myself in a thick duvet and fell into a blissful sleep.

CHAPTER TWENTY-SIX

I gazed at the reflection of the rays of the morning sun on the ocean, and took a sip of aromatic herbal tea. Sunday had come around again and it would soon be time to leave for the market.

I finished my tea, took one more look at the ocean and stepped out from the cottage. Something rustled beneath my feet. I instinctively looked down and saw a little white envelope. I placed my things carefully on the sand, and picked the envelope up with shaking hands.

Across the back, in a spidery hand, was written:

'For you, my dear Christina.'

The only clue I had as to who this was from was the thumping of my heart. I ripped the envelope open and pulled out the letter within.

Dear Christina,

You cannot know the breadth of my love for you, and I cannot deny its power. However, I respect your decision for us to only ever be friends. Therefore, I must disappear from your life forever. It is better this way. I simply cannot go on hiding my feelings from the world for you anymore. If I stayed, I would only cause you pain and torment. My leaving will save you from this suffering.

Tears fell from my eyes like rain. I wiped them away and continued to read.

Know you have been the source of the sweetest happiness in my life, my dear Christina. I will never forget the taste of your lips when we kissed for the first time. It felt like touching the first flower of spring.

Beautiful lady, you turned so many grim days into a forever shining realm of dreams. I will never forget seeing you that first time, looking for Marina. The light in your eyes and the extraordinary beauty of your soul will remain in my heart the rest of my days.

When I found you on the beach a month later, I was unaware how cruel the days had treated you.

The moment I realised that you were a poor street artist, my heart burst for you. I offered you money, but you were too proud to accept it, so I helped you to sell your paintings. Did you know that? I bought them all.

I knew there was something familiar about that man. I knew it. Part of me was so angry reading what Martin had done – pretending to like my pictures just to give me some money – but his heart was so good I could not be angry for long.

I read on.

When I saw the happiness in your eyes, my heart burst once more – but this time out of joy. I always tried to make you happy in my company. I hope that you felt it.

I wish you all the very best. Go for your dreams, my beautiful soul. I will always remember your sweet face and what it felt just to be with you.

Do not look for me. I am leaving for Lima and the hometown of my mother, tonight. I have some projects there waiting for me. Do not worry. I will never be far from your heart. Just say a morning prayer to the sun like the flowers do, and I will be there, smiling to you, hiding behind the silver cloud.

I love you.
Forever yours,
    Martin

The letter dropped from my hand. Large tears trickled down my cheeks, soon becoming a flood.

As the tears began to dry, my anger surfaced.

He was leaving me just when I need him the most? What kind of friend does that? He was nothing but a selfish liar – like all men. If they do not get the love from a woman they demand as their right, they disappear. They might dress it all up in words of love, but they are cowards.

My thoughts slowed, and I was overcome by a great sadness. I gave him love in the best way I could – as a friend. And that was not enough for him.

I sat on the sand, my back hard against the closed door, my sobbing growing louder and louder.

After, I know not how long, my mind tuned in to the melody of the waves beating against the shore. My heart had sunk in sorrow, but it had not yet turned to stone.

And what about you, Christina? the little voice sounded inside me.

'What about me?' I said out loud, not caring who heard.

You know very well what. Place your hand on your heart. It knows only love.

I wiped the tears from my face and did as instructed by my deeper self. Waves of love engulfed me, embracing my body and my soul.

And I knew the love I felt in that moment was a love for all time.

CHAPTER TWENTY-SEVEN

Marina came to me early the next morning. She grabbed my hand and with tears in her eyes.

'I know. He has gone,' she whispered.

'How do you know?' I asked.

'He came to say goodbye.'

'To you? But–'

I could not hide my disappointment.

Marina bit her lip.

'You mean to say he did not come to see you before he left?' she said. 'Then how do you know he has gone, Christina?'

I handed Marina the letter.

Tears filled her eyes as she read it to the end.

Marina handed the letter back to me with a heavy sigh.

'He is so much in love with you, Christina,' she said. 'Please try to understand him.'

'Understand him?' I hissed through gritted teeth. 'Understand him? What about me? Did he consider how I would feel? Playing at being friends when all the time he was just trying to seduce me? And he calls that love?'

'He loves you, Christina.'

I couldn't breathe. My head was spinning. I went over to the open window for some air, and caught sight of the restless sea, dancing and jumping and threatening. Once I managed to breathe more regularly, I returned to Marina.

'I really do not understand what you are trying to say,' I said. 'It sounds like you are defending him. He said he would be my friend, Marina, no matter what. Then just because his love is not returned, he runs off to the other side of the world!'

Marina marched towards me and waved Martin's letter in my face.

'Stop behaving like a little girl!' she yelled. 'Do you not see? Have you not considered his feelings? He loves you, Christina! *He loves you!* I watched his eyes dance in madness when he spoke of you. I know your project is important, you are becoming self-reliant, your ex-husband hurt you in the past, but this man, *this man* comes to you and professes his love and you turn your back?'

Tears rolled down my cheeks.

'Oh, Chris,' Marina said, her tone soft and sweet as she wrapped her arms around me.

'I am not scared of anything,' I said, the words almost consumed by sobs. 'I just want to live.'

'*You* are denying *yourself* the permission to live, Christina. The little you inside, she is scared. Give her love. Embrace her, Christina. Listen to her.'

The sobs came thick and fast now as I sobbed into Marina's shoulder.

'Listen to her, Christina,' she whispered. 'Listen to her.'

And I knew she was right.

CHAPTER TWENTY-EIGHT

I saw Martin in my dreams, standing in the centre of a large meadow, tall grass all around. His face was radiant. He stretched his arms towards me. How I wanted to approach him and embrace him, but a strange force held me back.

'I love you,' he said.

His words echoed in my soul.

I stretched my arms towards him.

But he was gone.

I scurried through the meadow, trying to find him. I called to him, but there was no answer. I ran wildly, madly till I stumbled over a large stone. I uttered a mighty cry and collapsed to the ground. *You will find him*, I said to myself. *You will find him*. But I no longer had the strength in my legs to stand.

And the hollowness of the night dragged on.

I called desperately for Martin, choking on my tears.

This was how I awoke, tears of loss and grief streaming down my face.

I turned on the bedside lamp and thought of doing some drawing to ease my pain. After a few sketches, I stretched, I yawned and I slept till I felt the morning sun dancing upon my cheeks, as if to invite me to start the day.

But my numb soul did not want to play along. I curled up and buried my face in my pillow and sank deeper into the mattress. When I eventually dragged myself from my bed, my eyes were swollen with the tears I had shed, and my body was stiff and aching. I craved the wide-open spaces of the beach and so threw on some clothes and left the cottage without eating breakfast.

I strolled along the sand, observing the restless sea.

'Why did you do that to me, Martin?' I said to no one, staring blank at the waves crashing onto the shore.

Pebbles ripped into my bare feet as I walked. When I could stand the pain no more, I stopped walking and sat on the sand to tend my wounds. A steady stream of blood trickled from several cuts. I took a tissue from my pocket and dipped it in the sea. Applying the wet compress, the saltiness of the water gnawed on my cuts causing even more pain. With one hand pressing the compress, I freed the other hand to wipe the tears. Words started to spill from my soul.

How could you leave me, Martin? How can a friend do that? I hate you for this.

Tears poured down my cheeks. I sat like that for hours, hoping Martin would come.

I watched the sunset and my body shivered.

I had no wish to go back home.

'Home?' I said out loud. 'Where is home?'

I must have asked this question thousands of times before.

When an empty heart plays tricks on you and there is no space in it to love yourself, let alone others, home is a mere illusion.

'Shush, you stupid little voice. Why are you telling me this nonsense? Do you not see how much I suffer?'

In truth, I disliked myself for the way I had treated Martin. I had acted like a cold bitch, not a woman. Even if I had wanted to be his friend only, I could have shown more feelings towards him. I could have at least been kind. A wave of fresh tears tried to fill up my eyes, but I held them back with all the strength I had left in me.

'To hell with feelings!' I hissed through my teeth.

The sky grew darker. I looked up at the golden contours of the moon carved into the black canvas of the night. This is not a night for seagulls, I thought.

More bitterness crept into my heart.

He couldn't even say goodbye to me in person. He is nothing but a coward. A self-centred coward. Marina said it broke his heart to leave, but she knows nothing about love, nothing about friendship.

I sighed heavily, and placed both my hands over my breaking heart in the vain hope of holding it together.

CHAPTER TWENTY-NINE

As the day began, I dragged my body from the bed and I looked at my puffy eyes in the mirror after another sleepless, merciless night.

I tried to smile to myself.

But I could not.

'Where has that beautiful face gone?' I asked, patting my cheeks with affection.

I hoped the little voice inside would speak to me as usual, as it often did in moments like this. But this time, there was nothing. I could not stand this silence. I could not stand these long days. They stretched themselves without end. Even the hours I spent painting hardly filled the void. I longed for the sweetness of Martin's voice. My hunger for his touch was immeasurable.

'Someone must know where exactly Martin is,' I murmured to myself.

I put on the best dress I had in my wardrobe, and started for Sofía's house. I had to start somewhere.

My feet were light across the sand, though still sore from the cuts on my soles.

I did not look back.

As I approached Sofía's house, I hesitated before stepping forward and pressing the doorbell. To the left of the door a big rose bush swayed delicately in the air.

I grabbed two beautiful roses in my hands and greedily inhaled the scent.

A voice from behind startled me.

'¡Hola Christina!'

I turned quickly.

And there stood the Seagull Boy wearing his school uniform and carrying a school bag.

'Hello, my dear. How are you?' I said. 'It has been such a long time.'

'I am okay. I have to go to school now. My nanny is inside if you want to talk to her,' he said, and waved a goodbye before hurrying up the path.

Before I managed to say another word, the Seagull Boy had disappeared.

I felt compelled to smell the roses again as if I wanted to take the whole lot of them with me. I turned round to do so, and watched a beautiful bee sitting just in the centre of one of the roses absorbing its nectar. My eyes looked in wonder, and I felt my mind drift slowly away.

The sweet voice of Sofía sounded from above, calling down through an open window. I looked up and smiled.

'They are beautiful, aren't they?' Sofía said. 'I will come down. Wait a minute.'

In what seemed like seconds, the door opened and there stood Sofía.

'What a surprise, Christina!' she said, a wide grin upon her face. 'Come here, my dear.'

Sofía pulled me towards her and wrapped her arms around me.

'Stand back,' she said, 'stand back. Let me look at you.'

I did as she requested, a little shy at being examined in this way.

'My, you are so beautiful, Christina,' she said. 'Now, you must come in and tell me everything.'

Sofía said to me to take a seat on the sofa whilst she went into the kitchen to make a cup of tea for us both. I sat there in silence, examining the walls, wondering how to ask her about Martin. A beautiful antique clock hung above the fireplace, its heavy hands slowly working around its big belly. I smiled grimly to myself, remembering the sound of the crushing waves of last night and how both the waves and this clock measured time so mercilessly.

Sofía returned with a tray brimming with home-made bread, fig jam, butter cookies and grapes. There was also a teapot with a crooked handle, the whole thing beautifully decorated with rose paint.

'Here you are,' she said, and laid the tray upon a little side-table.

I poured tea for myself and Sofía. It smelled wonderful.

'So, tell me, Christina, how is your arts project going? I have heard so much about it.'

I looked into Sofía's eyes. A beautiful light filled them, a certain quality I had no words for. I could have stared at them for hours. My lips twitched. I had not the energy for small talk. I had to know about Martin.

'Christina, are you okay? You did not answer my question. The arts project?'

I nodded, and almost answered, but the words would not come out and I broke into tears. Sofía moved to sit beside me, and placed her hands upon my lap.

'Whatever it is, my dear?' she said. 'I am here for you.'

She listened to my story of Martin without interference.

When I finished my story, I looked at her face, the tears trickling down her worn cheek, her grey hair spun tight around her fingers.

'It must have been hard for you to hear all that about Alejandro's mother again, Sofía. I am so sorry.'

'There is no thing worse in this life, Christina, than for a mother to lose her child.' She paused, and added, 'Especially for a mother who did not let her daughter marry the man she was madly in love with, and did not get the chance to say sorry.'

'It is not you who caused her death, Sofía,' I said.

'It is true, Christina, I did not kill her. But she spent her final years in misery because of me. My forceful opinions and behaviour killed her long before she died in that car crash. She married a man she did not love – because of me. She gave birth to Alejandro very soon – and Alejandro really was the shining light that kept her going for as long as she did – but to lose Martin as she did, she never got over that. And she never forgave me for it. Oh, my precious daughter, my child,' she whimpered, and crossed her hands on her chest as if trying to hold her breath.

Large tears flooded her face once more.

'Please do not blame yourself, Sofía.'

Sofía nodded, dabbed her wet eyes with a handkerchief, and continued:

'It must have been heart-breaking for Martin to see my daughter marry a different man, let alone see her give birth to the child. That is what hurt him the most. He always spoke of one day having a child when he was with my daughter, but it wasn't to be. As Alejandro grew, I saw the pain in Martin's eyes whenever he saw him, yet he never found the courage to speak to the boy. Alejandro is the image of his mother, you see.'

'That is so sad,' I said.

'Martin is such a beautiful man, Christina,' Sofía continued. 'He does not deserve such pain, whereas I…'

I pressed her hand as she broke down and held her to me as if she were a child.

'We can never undo what was once done, Christina. Evil possessed my soul and I have been punished.' Sofía let out a long, deep breath. 'Now,' she said, 'let's focus on you and Martin. You love him, don't you?'

I did not know what to say. My lips were restless to speak words of comfort to Sofía, but all I could think of was Martin and the further pain I had caused him.

All I could think of was myself.

'We cannot undo what we have once done, Sofía,' I said. 'All we can do is hope not to cause such pain again.'

Sofía appeared to settle at these words, and her sobbing began to ease.

'Do you love him, Christina?' she said again. 'Martin?'

I blushed at the very thought of him.

'Life is happening *now*, Christina. We do not get a second chance. I messed up the life of my own daughter and lost her love forever. Please, do not make the same mistake with Martin. You know what to do.'

I narrowed my eyes, remembering Marina telling me the same thing not so long ago.

'Do you know where he is, Sofía?' I asked softly.

Sofía shook her head. Nobody knew where Martin was. It was as if in the blink of an eye, he no longer existed.

When I arrived home that night, I couldn't even bring myself to look in the mirror. In any case, who would I see? A woman who had lost touch with the most beautiful human being she had ever known all because she was too selfish and too afraid to love?

I would have cried all the rivers of this world, if there were any tears inside me left to cry.

But even they had deserted me.

CHAPTER THIRTY

The days passed. Everything went back to normal. The project was ready, the venue refurbished. The workshops began. I opened the exhibition of my own paintings in an old school, all the money from their sale going to causes supporting other artists and a local homeless charity. I had also accepted a part–time position as an art teacher in an English high school in Gran Canaria. In addition, I continued with my stall in the market selling paintings and little sculptures that I learnt to carve out of wood or clay. It was a busy time and I even earned enough to consider moving house.

Marina was very supportive. She did not mention Martin to me after that first time. I often saw her lost in her own thoughts and wondered if she was secretly trying to find out where he had gone and to bring him back to Spain.

On a beautiful evening, I stood on the pier gazing out at the ocean, lost in thoughts of Martin. As if from another world, I felt his breath on the back of my neck as he kissed it gently. With my heart about to burst, I turned to face him.

But it was not Martin.

'What the hell are you doing here?' I yelled.

Philip's eyes were full of sadness.

'I have found you, Chris. Finally!'

He went to embrace me, and I backed away.

Philip smiled and clasped his hand and looked deeply into my eyes.

My lips quivered.

'But how? I do not understand. How?' I said.

'Does it matter, Chris? Aren't you happy to see me?'

He took a step towards me and I backed away a little further still.

'Happy? What should I be happy about?'

'After what you went through here, I thought you would be glad of a friendly face. I've missed you, Chris. If you can just give me a chance to at least talk to you.'

My knees trembled. Visions of my past life with Philip exploded in my mind like a scene from a battlefield. I opened my mouth to speak, but my lips were cracked and dry and the words came out harsh and unfeeling.

'You blamed me for ruining our marriage. Now you want to talk about it! I am sick and tired of all your games, Philip.'

He lowered his eyes like a repentant child.

'Don't tell me you didn't miss me a little?' he said, quietly.

'And if I say, I didn't?' I said.

My heart shrank as I watched him stand there in so much pain, and I offered him my hand.

He touched it with such tenderness.

'You are so beautiful, Christina. May I touch your face?' he asked gently.

I examined him closely. He had more of a gentle look on his face than I remember, his beard was no more and his hair was longer. His posture was bent and his legs were so skinny I was surprised they could hold him up at all.

'Philip,' I said, taking a deep breath, 'why are you here? Our story is over. Do you not understand? I am trying to be nice to you, as I appreciate that you travelled a long way, but there is nothing for you here.'

He looked deep into my eyes. A tear rolled down his cheek. He crossed his arms on his chest and whispered. 'But Chris, you are in my heart.'

A sea of compassion surged through me. I took a step closer to him, and wiped the tear from his face.

'Perhaps we can talk,' I said, unable to bear his pain anymore.

I was not sure I was doing the right thing inviting Philip to my cottage, but it felt like we needed somewhere to talk. I went straight to the bathroom and washed my face, bringing a short relief to my face burnt by the scorching heat of the day.

When I returned, Philip was sitting in my armchair, seemingly lost in thought.

An awkward silence fell between us, one I eventually broke.

'Who told you I was here, Philip? Was it Marina?'

He shifted in his seat a little.

'I promised not to tell,' he mumbled.

The same old Philip – the eternal keeper of secrets.

'Please, Chris, can't we just us talk about us?'

'There is no *us*, Philip. There has been no *us* for a very long time.'

I swallowed the saliva that had built up in my mouth, and I turned my face away from him.

'But you brought me here. There must be some feelings for me in your heart, Christina. There must.'

Thoughts and feelings churned inside my mind. All the wounds I thought had healed, now reopened, itching terribly. Words I had said to Philip over the years replayed in my mind, biting me like a venomous serpent, tearing me apart. I started to lose my breath, battling with myself and with the monster I had given life to inside my soul.

'Are you okay, Christina?' he said, with such gentleness.

My heart beat with such ferocity. Words got stuck in my throat. I reached in my pocket and took out a small tissue to wipe my sweating face. And we sat there in silence. A million buried feelings I could no longer ignore surging to the surface.

'I was brave enough to chase after my dreams, Philip, but I was never brave enough to tell you how I truly felt.'

Philip moved to sit next to me on the settee. He put his arm around my shoulders, and I leaned into him.

'I loved you so much once, Philip,' I whispered, swallowing my tears.

'I loved you Chris,' he replied, 'and I still…'

118

He hesitated a little, and then running his fingers through my hair, he said, 'There is still a place for you in my heart, my dear Christina. It took you to leave for me to understand you, and to understand myself.'

'I could not make myself happy, Philip. How could I have ever made you?'

'You can now,' he said.

'But I choose not to Philip. I choose not to.'

I closed my eyes and felt him lift off the settee, his heavy footsteps treading towards the door.

And he was gone.

CHAPTER THIRTY-ONE

The beach lost its form as I ran with all the force I had left in my legs. My body and my soul ached. My mind raced. I had to stop. I looked up at the endless blue. Oh, how I wanted to soar into the sky like a seagull and leave all my pain behind.

Breathless, I plodded trough the small alley leading to Marina's house. The trees danced in the wind, the soft music of their rustling leaves calming me. Marina was in her front garden when I arrived. On seeing me, she dropped everything, and ran to greet me. We hugged, and in her arms I felt safe and welcome.

'Are you okay, darling?' she whispered to my ear.

'Philip is back,' I said. 'It is like my past is haunting me. I thought it was over.'

I looked at Marina's face. Her big hazel eyes stared at me. She looked beautiful as usual, but there was something deep within those big hazel eyes I couldn't quite grasp.

I drew back from her.

'Was it you who told him where I lived, Marina?'

Marina turned her face away from me. 'Chris. I…' her voice broke.

I could hear a soft cracking sound coming from a nearby house. The wind blew on my face, and I suddenly felt trapped.

'So, it was you?'

Her lips opened and then closed, as if she did not know how to form the words she wished to say.

'Yes, I told him,' she finally said. 'I know I shouldn't have, Christina, but he begged me. He was in so much pain.'

'I thought you would bring Martin back to me, Marina, not Philip.'

'And what did you think? That Martin would come back after you made it clear you did not want him? If you have the right to cast the hurt from your life, Christina, and move on, then surely he has the right to do the same!'

Her words stung me and I felt such a wrenching pain inside.

'But, Marina, you knew I was not ready for an intimate relationship with any man, and yet you brought Philip here? And I thought you were my closest friend?'

Marina had nothing more to say.

CHAPTER THIRTY-TWO

When I arrived home, Philip was there, waiting for me on the steps of the cottage. His face was radiant as he handed me a rose.

And part of me, the part longing once again to be loved, melted inside.

We strolled along the beach in silence, the waves playfully touching our feet. The cool breeze kissed my cheeks leaving me in a strong need of more kisses. I lifted my skirt and waded into the vast waters of the ocean. In the music of the sea I lost all my worries. All the bad memories I ever had dissolved in the waves. Philip watched me from the shore.

The sea grew in its power, roaring and spluttering. I went back to the shore. Philip was still there. I was wet and shaking from the cold. He put his blazer on me and pulled me closer to him.

'Christina,' he said, softly, 'we need to get you dry.'

'You have changed, Philip. What happened?'

'For you, Chris,' he murmured. 'All for you.'

I closed my eyes, and he slowly drew me into his arms and stroked my hair. Philip planted a kiss first on my cheeks and then on my lips.

My body was reluctant, at first, but I quickly fell into his embrace.

'I need to change,' I whispered. 'I am soaking wet.'

We walked back to the cottage.

The light of the moon streamed through my bedroom window, shining upon our naked bodies entwined. His lips landed softly on mine showering them with kisses, his hands stroking every inch of my sea water body.

I responded to each single caress with soft murmuring.

There was nothing to hide in this moment. Subtle kisses turned into more passionate ones. Their intensity pleased me.

And I was laid open again to a man that had once hurt me.

Can reconciliation be achieved in this way? Can old wounds ever be healed? These thoughts passed through my mind as I tried to tune into the melody of two bodies merging into one.

CHAPTER THIRTY-THREE

The next morning I awoke, and Philip was not beside me. I called his name, but there was no response. I walked to the bathroom. It was empty. I caught my reflection in the bathroom mirror. What have you done, Christina? I thought. Are you not ashamed? I looked down at my body with revulsion.

The little voice spoke:

Christina, do not get upset with yourself. No matter what you do I am always by your side.

'Even if it is a stupid thing? 'I replied.

Especially if it is a stupid thing. Whatever happened last night, there is no reason to hate yourself.

But I was not loyal.

To whom you were not loyal? the little voice asked.

To everyone. To myself. To Martin.

Martin? You said he was just your friend.

Yes. I did.

Tell me, Christina, how disloyal have you really been to Martin? Be honest with yourself. You alone know the truth.

Large, silent tears ran down my cheeks. I indulged in their saltiness on my lips, swollen from yesterday's kisses.

CHAPTER THIRTY-FOUR

Marina visited me in the afternoon. I sat in a little corner of my room clutching at the curtains.

'I am so sorry, Christina,' Marina said. 'I know I shouldn't have invited Philip to Gran Canaria. But you told me you don't care about him. Just send him back to London. He will understand. He is a mature man.'

I buried my face in my hands and felt the darkness surrounding me, the same darkness that consumed me when I was at the hospital. A debilitating darkness. a malicious darkness.

'Christina! Are you listening to me? Am I talking to the wall?'

Marina came close to me and put her hands on my shoulders.

'It is easy, honey. Just tell him. You don't need him, do you?'

My eyes shed a few tears. Swallowing them with a great difficulty I told her what happened.

'Marina, I made love to him last night.'

'But… I don't understand. Do you care for him now?'

A loud sobbing came out from the deepest layers of my soul.

She tried to read from my face.

'You love him, then?'

'No, I don't,' I blurted out, shaking myself free from her grasp. I sank against the wall. 'It just happened. He was so nice. I hadn't seen him like that for so long.'

She drew me into her arms, stroking my head and rocking me slightly from side to side as my mother once did.

'How can I look at my face in the mirror after what I have done, Marina?'

'Did you speak to him about it afterwards?'

'No. He left before I awoke.'

'It was probably hard for him to face you. He must have sensed you would not be willing to reconcile.'

I knew she was right. Philip never could face the truth.

'Marina,' I said. 'Thank you for coming.'

Marina pulled me close and kissed my cheeks.

And my broken soul felt comforted, for just a while.

CHAPTER THIRTY-FIVE

I was working on a painting on the beach when I heard Philip's voice.

'Christina! There you are.'

My eyes remaining glued to the painting.

'I know you don't want to speak to me, Chris. I acted like a coward that night, leaving you as I did.'

I stopped mixing my paint and looked up into his eyes.

'We should not have done what we did, Philip.'

'Chris, how can you be so tough with me? After such a beautiful night?'

'Do you mean as tough as me waking up in the morning alone. As tough as that?' I retorted.

'Chris, I am sorry. I…'

'You have always been a coward, Philip. It was not the first time you left me like that. You have not changed at all.'

The seagulls circled around our heads. Their shrieking deafened me. I stood speechless, gazing at Philip. He came forward and grabbed my hands.

'Please, forgive me,' he said.

He bit his lower lip and came closer still. 'You are so beautiful and so incredibly strong. I realise that now.'

'Marina told you, didn't she?' I said, looking directly into his eyes. 'She told you how to find me.'

'She told me the whole story, Chris. She said how you had *reached for your dreams*.'

He said this with the bitterness and sarcasm of old, as if my dreams were the dreams of a child.

'But what is life,' Philip continued, 'if it is only *your* goals you pursue? Life is also about love and sharing that love with others.'

'And I perfectly understand that, Philip. I am truly giving all I have inside. I am happy I am making this world a better place.'

'I am talking about love between a woman and man, Chris. *Real* love.'

'You will never understand me, Philip. And I do not need you to.'

'But Chris,' he moaned.

'Goodbye, Philip,' I said, and left him standing alone on the beach.

The days passed, and Philip still had not got the message. I would see him around the market when I was there at the stall with my paintings, or strolling along the beach gazing at the sky whenever I crossed the sand. The clouds grew darker whenever I saw him.

Why was it so hard for him to understand? I was hardly eating. I could not concentrate on my arts project. It even came to the point where I wondered about returning to London, just to be rid of him. But I knew Philip would simply follow.

I began to think of Martin. Was he ever to return to Spain or had I really driven him away? He had his animal shelter to run here. His life was here. *I* was here. And Marina? Where I could find a better friend than her? I know she didn't act reasonably bringing Philip here. But everyone makes mistakes. She is a good-hearted person.

But most of all, my thoughts centred on me. What did *I* want? What did I *really* want?

These questions were hard to answer. I forever placed my hands upon my heart for guidance, but none would come but a few small words echoing in the darkness:

Be good to yourself, said the voice.

How can I be good to myself when I feel so broken?

Just be, the voice said.

No more words came out from this little voice, the only friend I had in the whole world – apart from Marina.

The evening of the art exhibition arrived, and my hands trembled at the thought of leaving the cottage. Philip would probably be waiting for me on the pier or the sand, or at the exhibition itself. There would be no escape from that man. For weeks I had felt a prisoner in my own home. How I missed the clear blue days when I would run free on the beach and dance with the waves. I so pitied myself and my lost freedom.

All my life I had not had the guts to express my feelings in the most crucial moments. I had told Philip how I felt, but this had not been enough. There was so much I held back, so much pain, so much hurt.

But there was one thing I was sure of.

Philip was not for me.

I remember promising myself when I arrived in Gran Canaria, I would not fall in love again. And then Martin came along.

All those beautiful memories came to my mind, all at once, at the thought of him. Our strolls along the beach, our first kiss, the softness of his touch, his kindness, his passion.

I looked at my reflection in the mirror, and how my face glowed at these thoughts of him. I put my hand on my heart and felt it throbbing tirelessly within my little body – and dreamed of it throbbing against his.

I could hide it from myself no longer.

I was in love with Martin.

I opened the door to the cottage, my heart ablaze with love, and there stood Philip, his gaze full of concern.

'I am a coward, Chris,' he said, the tears rolling down his face. 'I want to change but I cannot do it alone. You are the only one who can help me. I love you, Chris.'

His huge green eyes stared at me.

I was speechless. I reached for his hand and squeezed it gently. We stood like that for a long time.

As the sun began to set it spilled its beautiful range of colours across the canvas of the sky.

I wished I had the courage to do the same. The courage to speak my thoughts. The courage to speak the truth. I had called Philip a coward many times.

But I was a coward too.

CHAPTER THIRTY-SIX

Many days, many moods, many shapes of clouds passed. Philip still hung around the beaches of Gran Canaria like a shadow.

Everything was as it should be, I told myself. I had no plans. I had no resolutions – apart from one: to be free.

I learnt not to attach myself to the feelings of sadness or joy. Instead, I placed my burden in the loving hands of Mother Earth, and waited. What I was actually waiting for, I had no idea.

I spent my days painting, no longer being careful about my techniques, but just transferring the messy thoughts and feelings churning inside me onto the canvas. No censorship, no self-judgement. Just freedom. Total freedom.

Abstract ideas replaced beautiful contours. Where once I had painted detailed pictures of human beings or houses, now a myriad of colours danced joyfully upon my canvas.

And I was content with what I saw. It was not perfect, but it was me.

I missed Marina, but I did not want to disturb her. Her husband had returned from Peru, and they needed time together. She invited me to her house for dinner several times, but I knew it was only out of politeness – a sense of duty.

We had not seen each other for a while, myself and Marina, when one afternoon on my return from the market, I found a note from her left on my kitchen table. She said she had to see me urgently.

I rushed down the path leading from the beach, through the little wood, and reached Marina's house as quick as I could, afraid something might have happened to her. Silence surrounded the little place. A blissful moment when I could hear only my heartbeat. I hesitated for a moment, and then pressed the doorbell.

Heavy footsteps approached the door. I peeped through the small window in the door to see who might be there. The figure was taller and bigger than Marina, so I knew it could not be her. When the door opened, a handsome man with tanned skin, hazel eyes and a very beautiful nose stood there. His eyebrows were furrowed and he wore a small beard. His hair was thick and dark, and impeccably styled.

'Hello,' he said. You must be Christina.'

With one gesture of his hand, he invited me inside the house. The smell of freshly baked biscuits was divine.

'Is Marina at home? I asked shyly.

'She is in the kitchen,' he said. 'She asked me to tell you to wait for her. Please make yourself at home.'

'Thank you,' I said, and took a seat on the sofa whilst Marina's husband – for it must have been him – reached for a small cupboard and took out three beautiful glasses, placing them on a sliver tray on the table.

'I won't be a moment,' he said, and retreated to the kitchen, emerging a few seconds later with a large glass jug.

'Lemon and orange mint water,' he said, placing the jug on the tray. 'Would you like some?'

I said that I would, and tried to force a smile, all the time wondering what the emergency might be.

Marina's husband filled my glass with the aromatic water, and handed it to me, then filled one for himself.

I marvelled at how gentlemanly his manners were. Marina was so lucky. She must have won her husband in the lottery, I thought, so perfect was he.

But everyone has their own story, their own joy, their own pain, all carved silently into their hearts. Who really knows the truth of another? At last, Marina entered the living room, and her husband excused himself, leaving the two of us alone.

The moment her husband left the room, Marina darted towards me.

'My dear, Christina!' she yelped, jumping happily towards me and wrapping me in her arms. 'I am so happy that you finally came. I have missed you so much. To be honest, I began to get a little bit worried when you kept refusing my invitations. I thought, you know, Philip… It is all my fault, Christina. I am so sorry.'

She collapsed onto the sofa, and I sat down beside her.

'Oh, hush Marina,' I said, grasping her hands. 'Sooner or later he would have turned up anyway. What is meant to be is meant to be.'

'He is a stubborn man, Christina. He must love you very much.'

There was a darkness around Marina's eyes, a limitless darkness that spoke of many sleepless nights.

'I have no love for Philip,' I said, the words coming out colder than I intended. 'I have compassion, but I have no love.'

Marina's face contorted into one of anger and confusion.

'Compassion, Christina? You still have compassion for him, even after he came here and used you like he did?'

'And I let him, Marina. Maybe I used him too, in some way. Please, Marina, this is not the time for blame. You said there was something urgent you needed to tell me.'

Just then, Marina's husband came back with a tray of small biscuits, their aroma filling the whole room. I looked at them with hungry eyes.

'Please,' Marina said. 'Help yourself.'

I reached greedily for one, and then took another. I popped one into my mouth. The biscuit melted on my tongue. My taste buds were in Heaven.

'Oh, Marina. These are delicious,' I said.

She laughed wholeheartedly, took a biscuit from the plate, dipped it in her tea and ate it.

'They're not bad,' she said, and blushed a little.

After a while, she reached for my hands and looking deeply into my eyes.

'Christina,' she said, 'I am going to be a mum.' A big smile spread across her face.

Tears fell from my eyes. 'That is wonderful news, Marina. I am so happy for you.' I wiped the tears with my hand. 'Is this the urgent news you wished to share?'

'I just didn't know how else to get you over here. I had to tell you in person.'

'My dearest friend,' I said, and knew not what else to say.

We hugged, and then Marina left for the kitchen to bring in some tea.

As I sat there alone, I wondered why the tears that appeared on my face felt like tears of sorrow. Marina was my friend, my best friend. So why tears of sorrow?

I put my hand on my belly. It was there. It was definitely there. A sorrow swelling to a gigantic size, demanding my attention.

Here Christina, said the little voice.

What? What are you trying to tell me?

Here, Christina, the voice sounded louder. *Here.*

I tried to feel with my hands this great sorrow now reaching such a size that I started to lose my breath. I imagined the sorrow sitting before my eyes, and it grew bigger and bigger. I watched how from the size of a seed this ball of sorrow reached the size of a large balloon. I watched it expand, with no judgement. I simply let it be. I tried to peer inside the balloon, but there was nothing to see. I imagined a big needle within my grasp, able to pop the balloon, to make it burst and disappear. I thought about grabbing the needle to do just this but, for some reason decided not to. The balloon of sorrow continued to grow to such a size, it filled the entire room. And when it could grow no more, I watched to my surprise as it gradually began to shrink until it became the size of a seed once more, and disappeared.

I felt a sort of relief in my soul.

Full of gratitude I placed my hands on my heart. Marina came back with a tray with two teas and a plate of sandwiches.

'I am sorry it took me so long,' she said. 'I guessed you must be hungry, so I prepared some food. Please help yourself.'

The sandwiches were as elegantly and delicately made as the small biscuits. And the tea tasted like the tea my mother used to make. For a moment, it really felt like all was as it should be.

'There is one more thing I need to tell you,' Marina said.

Her face changed to the colour of deepest red, and her words were hesitant. She looked in the direction of her husband, now standing in the kitchen doorway.

'Okay,' I said, realising what she was about to say was the real reason she had asked me over.

'As you already know, Christina, I am pregnant,' she said. Her words sounded clumsy in her mouth, as if they were unformed until the moment she gave them life. As if there was something else she wanted to tell me, but did not know how. 'We went through quite an ordeal with my mum-in-law's condition,' she continued. 'We thought we would lose her, and that would have destroyed my husband. He loves her so much and feels so bad that she can't be with us. She lives so far.'

She tried to avoid looking at me now.

'What is it, Marina? Just tell me,' I said.

'We need to sell the summer cottage,' she said. 'I am so sorry. We need the money from the sale to build an extension to our house so my husband's mother can live with us.'

I looked at her face, so full of worry.

'Marina, my dear friend. Sooner or later, I expected this. I cannot live out the rest of my days in a summer cottage, can I?'

I chuckled, and Marina chuckled too.

'I suppose not,' she said.

'I will manage. With the workshops, a part-time teaching position and my paintings, I have more money now. I thank you for all your kindness. Now, you need to think about yourself. You have a baby coming. Do not forget that!'

As I said these words a stinging pain crept across my heart. I looked back on all those mornings in the cottage, how it was there I learnt to be strong, to be self-reliant. This cottage had such an important place in my story. Hell, that cottage *is* my story. If the cottage went, it felt like a piece of me was to be sold along with it.

'I am so glad you understand,' Marina said. 'We have potential buyers lined up already. You do not need to worry, though, Christina. You can stay with us until you find somewhere.'

'Thank you. I can manage,' I said. 'I will look for a room this afternoon.'

'Are you sure? You really are more than welcome to stay with us until you find something, Christina.'

'I will be fine. If you could just give me a week.'

Marina's husband cut in.

'It will take some time to arrange for my mother to come from Peru,' he said. 'Would a month be better?'

'A week would be fine,' I said.

Marina suddenly collapsed on my shoulders, sobbing.

CHAPTER THIRTY-SEVEN

I would miss the summer cottage so much. I looked around the tiny kitchen lit by the faint light, then moved to the small living room I had spent so much time in since my homelessness came to an end in Gran Canaria. Then returned to the kitchen to look out of the window at the ocean. I would miss the sound of waves crushing against the shore, waking me up every morning, awakening also the truth of who I was.

With trembling fingers, I opened the window. The cool familiar breeze quickly entered and filled up my lungs with hope and strength.

Part of me didn't want to leave the cottage at all, but another part – a bolder part – knew it was time to reach for more.

I knew it was time again to speak to Philip, but I would not chase after him. When the time was right, I would know.

My body relaxed as I looked at the sea.

Now! said the voice.

'What now?' I murmured.

I opened my heart to listen, but the voice was gone. Instead I heard a myriad of noises coming from the sea – grunting, moaning, sighing noises, as if the sea itself were in pain.

I shivered.

It was time.

I found Philip sitting on the shore; his face buried in his hands. I approached, and called his name softly. He didn't move. I looked at the sea. It was calm, content I answered its call. I was at peace.

'Philip?' I repeated.

He turned to face me. His face was red, his eyes swollen. I could not bear his suffering. I put my arm on his shoulder.

'Philip, I…' my voice trembled, 'I am sorry. What took place that night in the cottage should not have happened. I apologise.'

He looked deep into my eyes, and remained silent. We sat there together till the first moonlight.

'Chris,' he finally spoke to me. 'I have something to tell you.'

He turned to face me and placed his hands on mine. My heartbeat accelerated. My hands started to sweat.

'I am going back to London, Chris. I am taking a flight tomorrow in the early morning.'

I watched his body as it trembled. 'Why did you not tell me from the beginning?'

'Tell you what?' I said, genuinely confused.

'The truth, Chris. The truth.'

I knew he meant Martin. How he found out, I had no idea.

'Does your heart beat faster for him than for me, Chris?'

'Yes, Philip,' I said, my voice trembling. 'It does.'

He released his hand from mine.

'Do not ask me if I am fine, Chris. I am torn apart. But I will let you go. You deserve the best.'

He planted a kiss on my cheek.

I had tears in my eyes. My body shrank and words never to be said got stuck in my throat.

'Be happy,' he said.

And that was the last thing I ever heard him say.

I stood on the shore, motionless. I still couldn't believe what had happened. I stayed there for a while listening to the crushing waves. They seemed to take the moon in their arms as I watched its reflection. I breathed in and out. All was silent, apart from the waves. There was a sadness at the bottom of my heart. And instead of pushing it away as

I had always done, I indulged it. I wallowed in it. I drowned in it.

And I was free.

CHAPTER THIRTY-EIGHT

I had enough money saved for a deposit on a decent small flat, and Gustavo and Sofía had promised to help me in my search. I was calm these days, content that I had my friends around me – even though my situation was precarious.

Sometimes, I thought of Martin but I no longer felt the sense of regret and loss I once did even though the warm feelings for him in my heart never left. I was happy Philip had finally understood he and I were not meant for each other, and his return to London was a huge relief.

As well as searching for a new place to live, my days were filled with a variety of errands – sending invitations for my exhibition and informing other artists of our project. My workshops began to attract impressive numbers, and I was happier now than I had been for as long as I could remember.

You won, girl, the voice inside me sounded triumphantly, no longer the little voice it once was, but a voice clear and pure.

'Thanks to you,' I said, and placed my hand upon my heart.

Ever since I was a little girl, I have learnt of the fragility of things, that nothing lasts forever. The serious illness and the unexpected death of my mum taught me that life is a constant battle.

The thought of leaving my little cottage did not hurt anymore. Tears sprang to my eyes, but the pain had eased. Life is about the coming and the going. There were people and places and opportunities waiting for me, and it was time for me to go and find them.

It was scorching hot these days. Whatever the sun took in its arms, it burnt. The grass, the flowers, the trees, the skin of lovers on the beach all were marked with scars from the sun. I used to carry those same scars in my soul. Hatred and unforgiveness do that, but the cool cleansing sea will always remind me that love rushing through the open channels of the heart can achieve miracles.

I always seemed to have been led down the paths that offered me growth. In spite of the pain and the torment I experience there, I have a deep gratitude for the experiences of my life.

The day I went to view my first flat, though, serious doubts crept into my heart, and I briefly considered going back to London. But Gran Canaria had engraved such beautiful images on my mind and heart, these thoughts left me as quickly as they had come.

Gustavo, as promised, took me to his friend's house – the owner of the flat – and we proceeded from there. The road was bumpy and seemed to have no end, as roads often do.

'Can we go a little faster?' I said, eager to begin my new life.

Gustavo's friend smiled.

'In Gran Canaria you learn how not to be annoyed with bumps in the road,' he said. 'They are all just part of the journey.'

'This is true,' Gustavo said, nodding his head wisely. 'This is true.'

Life reveals new lessons every day, and I knew this was another I had to learn to embrace.

I pressed my forehead against the window and watched the seagulls floating in the air. I recalled the days the Seagull Boy told me their stories, and realised I had not seen him for so long.

We passed under a beautiful bridge stretching itself across the road, and a family of geese strolling across it. Mango, papaya and banana plantations lay before us, reminding me of the sweet cherry blossom from my childhood in my nanny's garden.

I thought of my family, and how they were no more. I thought of Marina, Sofía, the Seagull Boy and Gustavo.

'Good, kind people,' I whispered to myself, 'You are my family now.'

The voice of Gustavo brought me back from my musings.

'Hey Christina!' he said, pointing at a little house in the distance. 'Can you see what I can see?'

There was a house set back in the trees —and the wood it was made from simply gorgeous. Bright flowers of every colour grew in the front garden and looped round the front door.

'How lucky someone must be to live there,' I said.

Gustavo and his friend laughed.

'Then you are the lucky one, I guess,' Gustavo said, turning his head round to me.

I swallowed my saliva, 'I thought we were heading towards your friend's flat.'

'A true artist needs to work in a place such as this,' Gustavo replied.

We turned off the main road towards the little house, and Gustavo's friend parked outside as if he had done so a million times before.

'Out you come, my dear Christina,' Gustavo said. 'Come and see your new house.'

A rose bush burnt by the sun, leaned gracefully against the colourful little fence. A little swing swayed gently in the breeze, tied to a large tree. The house itself, though small, was bigger than my summer cottage. It reminded me of something from a fairy tale.

'I know it is not a big house,' Gustavo said, almost as if he were apologising. 'And it is a little out of the way, but I have left you a bicycle so you can get to the centre of the village quickly. I hope that is all okay?'

I expected a flat surrounded by artificial gardens, nosy neighbours and the sound of traffic day and night. Not in my wildest dreams did I expect to be living in a place like this.

I said thank you to Gustavo, the only words I could find.

'Rent is simple, Christina, it will not be much,' he said. 'The nearest market is about two miles away, and the coast is not far. You will still hear the seagulls.'

He smiled, knowing what this meant to me.

Gustavo guided me inside the house to a view of the sea from the living room window.

'Here you go, Christina, what do you think?'

'I am speechless, I…'

'Don't think too much whether to take it or not. My friend here is offering the lowest rent he can. He prefers you to rent it for a longer period of time rather than as a holidaymaker, so it is a big decision for you.'

'I understand,' I said. 'I will definitely take it. It is an incredibly beautiful place. I cannot believe how lucky I am. When will it be available?'

'You can move in whenever you want,' Gustavo's friend said. 'It is yours.'

CHAPTER THIRTY-NINE

Suitcase in hand, I wiped a tear from my cheek and closed the door of the little summer cottage behind me for the last time.

I walked along the beach and listened for the subtle sounds of the sea, and remembered the story the Seagull Boy had told me about the big monster of Gran Canaria locked away in a cave. Ever since the Seagull Boy told me the story, I always imagined the monster was locked away in a cave nearby. I could never precisely pinpoint where it was, but I *felt* it.

The Seagull Boy taught me stories never really end. They continue on in the imagination of the reader, or the listener.

It's just how it is, he said.

In my mind, the big monster realised the error of his ways and came to apologise to the residents of the island. But nobody wanted to believe him and thought he was conspiring against them. They had been hurt too much. One day the biggest storm ever to rise from the sea hit the island. The seagulls had gathered and tried to send the storm back from whence it came, but all their efforts were in vain. It was then that the monster appeared, and with all his strength he held back the enraged waters, protecting the island and its inhabitants, until the sea became a perfect stillness. The residents of the island were amazed by the monster's heroic act and invited him to live on the islands forever.

Was this the right ending? Was there another? I did not know.

I suppose we never do. All we know is the ending that seems right to us.

I had settled into my beautiful new house for a couple of weeks, when I thought it was time to visit Marina. I wanted to give her time with her husband, and not crowd her in the early stages of her pregnancy. This was their time, after all.

'So you haven't forgotten your old friend,' Marina said, opening the door and smiling broadly, wrapping her arms around my neck.

Her face was radiant and her belly had grown noticeably.

'How could I?' I whispered, leaning my face upon her shoulder.

Marina invited me inside. She seemed so happy, yet fragile. Life was growing inside her, a little soul inside her small body. How beautiful, oh, how…

Tears came to my eyes.

'Oh, Chris, please, do not cry. Drink your tea or you will cry both your eyes right out!'

She laughed, and came to sit next to me on the sofa, placing her warm hand on my shoulder.

'I am so glad you found your place, Chris,' she said.

I smiled through my tears, 'And Philip has gone,' I said.

Marina told me she knew, and smiled triumphantly.

I drew back from, looking at her suspiciously.

'How do you know?'

Marina raised her head up, and quietly said: 'I have spoken to him, Chris.'

I wondered how Philip had known about Martin. And now I knew. I should have felt angry at Marina. But she was my friend. She was only looking out for me, I guess.

'I brought him here,' Marina continued, 'and felt responsible for getting rid of him. If you loved him, Chris, of course I would not have interfered. But you don't. What else could I do?'

I sipped my tea, still not quite knowing whether to feel angry or grateful.

'I would never hurt you, Chris. You know that. If I did, I–'

'Oh, stop it Marina,' I said, and gave her a big hug. She needed it even more than me. She carried a little baby inside her, and they could both do without worrying about me.

'So he really has finally gone,' Marina said, at last.

'Yes,' I said. 'He's gone.'

'I am so proud of you, Chris. Now – tell me about your new flat.'

'It is actually a house,' I said. 'It is small, but it is so lovely.'

Marina's jaw dropped. 'A house! Christina, all you ever dreamed! That is a serious reason to celebrate. I insist you accompany me to dinner right now!'

'It's only a–'

'It is only a nothing, Christina! You are coming with me now!' and she began pulling me up from the sofa. 'Besides,' Marina continued, 'I am so hungry.' She patted her tummy and licked her lips. 'We both are,' she added with a wink.

I looked at Marina's baby bump and her puffy eyes, and I laughed harder than I had done in a very long time.

I waited as Marina put on her best dress. She looked stunning.

'Your turn,' she said, ushering me to her bedroom, and opening her wardrobe. 'Take your pick.'

Although I was a bit taller than Marina, the dress I chose fit my figure perfectly, and we walked out into the night, giggling like a couple of teenage girls off to a party.

The road meandered across town, seeming to take an eternity to reach our destination. We passed the beautiful beach, and out beyond it the waves danced in the cool breeze. The foam on the top of the waves came and went, shamelessly exposing the blue body of sea for just a moment before crashing upon the shore.

The restaurant was right on the beachfront. Marina parked up, and we went inside.

The smell of baked fish was incredible, and made my belly rumble. Each table was lit by a small candle and a posy of red roses. The seats were made of the best wood, intricately carved, and the tablecloths were white, embroidered with a beautiful rose pattern. Soft music played in the background.

We were guided to a table near the front window by a friendly waitress, and opened the menu card.

'They serve a variety of fish here,' Marina said, pouring over the menu. 'And their salads are stunning.'

'Are you sure you can eat fish?' I said.

'Why not? I am so hungry. And for the last three months everything I ate came straight back up. Let me enjoy myself, eh?' She licked her lips and shot me a mischievous grin.

I fancied the seabream casserole. It looked delicious.

When the waiter appeared, Marina ordered fish soup for herself and two big glasses of papaya juice. I ordered the casserole. Not even two minutes passed when two big glasses of fresh papaya juice sat before us.

'This is amazing,' I said, sipping the juice.

But Marina was transfixed by something behind me.

'Can you see what I can see,' Marina replied looking wide-eyed straight over my shoulder, her face turning instantly white. She put her hand on her mouth as if she'd just seen a ghost.

She leaned across the table towards me.

'Either I am crazy,' she whispered, 'or the guy sitting two tables along from us is Martin.'

I turned without thinking, and my heart stopped. This time it was my turn for the blood to drain from my face.

It really was Martin.

He was laughing with another man at the table. Although the entire restaurant was lit only by candles, there was no mistaking that laugh.

I turned round to Marina.

'I can't believe it,' she said, reaching forward to take hold of my hands. 'I can't believe it. What are you going to do?'

A voice cracked open the silence between us. Marina withdrew her hands from mine, as a beautiful wooden bowl of steaming casserole was placed before me.

'And for you, señora' the waiter said, referring to Marina, 'the fish soup.'

Marina thanked the waiter for us both, and we watched him disappear into the darkness.

We spent the rest of the meal in silence.

When we left, I did not look back.

The night sky was crystal clear. The shrieking of the seagulls was aggressive and loud, and it tore me apart.

CHAPTER FORTY

Marina had forgotten her bag and went back inside the restaurant to retrieve it. I waited outside, inhaling the fresh sea air.

I felt a warm hand on my shoulder, firm and strong.

I breathed in one final lungful of sea air, as if to steel myself, and turned slowly round. Martin looked so handsome in his blue shirt, its collar unbuttoned and his hair slicked back.

He smiled and looked into my eyes so tenderly.

'Where did you go, my dear Christina?' he said softly.

'Me?' I replied, trying not to fall apart at the sound of his voice. 'You are the one that disappeared, Martin.'

His voice seemed to get stuck in his throat.

I looked at this man and his glistening, beautiful eyes – so deep, and so full of meaning. I had seen the same light in them so many times before, like a lantern in a dark sleepless night guiding my wandering soul into the land of dreams.

Martin wrapped his arms around me, and I felt his warm tears run down my cheeks. My tears joined his in a steady stream of love, and our warm lips touched.

I saw Marina coming from the corner of my eye, then realising what was happening, she stepped back.

Martin sensed I might be about to pull away, and drew me closer. I felt his heartbeat on mine, and he brought his mouth to my ear.

'I am so sorry, Christina,' he whispered. 'I am so sorry.'

'Where have you been Martin?' I said, the words spoken through tears. 'Six months? No call, no letters. I thought–'

'I know, Christina. I know. I just needed some space.' His eyes narrowed, his chin dropped, 'I wanted you to love me. When you did not return my feelings, I–'

'I *did* return them, Martin. You did not feel? I was scared, but always deep in my heart I dreamt about you. Did you not see me in your dreams, searching, so desperately searching?'

Martin pulled me even closer, hugging me tight.

'I did, Christina. That is why I am here. I just arrived yesterday in the late evening, and the first thing I did in the morning was a walk to your cottage. But you were not there. I saw the shutters closed and a "For sale" sign. And I was so scared.'

A shiver came through his body right into to mine.

'Why were you scared?' I asked softly.

He looked at me with such fondness in his eyes.

'Christina. I thought you had gone back to London, with *him*. I thought I had lost you forever.'

It was my turn to hold him close, this man, this man so full of love.

CHAPTER FORTY-ONE

Martin's absence, at first unbearable, had become something I had got used to. How many days and nights had passed without him? How many seagulls had floated above the sea? How many stars had blinked their sleepy eyes and protected me while I slept during those bleak, lonely nights?

I will never know.

And now he was back.

I looked at myself in the mirror. A beautiful face stared back at me. A light shone in my eyes I alone knew the meaning of.

My heart thumped hard. I knew what I had to do.

I grabbed my nightgown and went outside. The pitch-dark sky stared at me. The cool wind embraced me like a lover. My body tuned into the spirit of the evening and I closed my eyes, drinking in the beauty of this moment. I delved deep into my soul, listening for the whisper of the little Christina that had been so long lost, so long silent.

The following day sank in an overflowing love of the sun. I finished my art workshop and was heading for home. Martin was coming to see my house. My heartbeat accelerated as I rode home on my bike, my cheeks red, my body sweating. A car slowed down alongside me.

'I was on my way to you,' Martin called out, a big grin plastered across his face. 'Do you need a ride? You look exhausted.'

'Thank you, Martin,' I said. 'That would be amazing.'

Martin pulled his car up onto the pavement and opened the passenger door.

I transferred my big bag of art equipment to the boot of Martin's car, and waited as Martin fixed my bike to the car roof.

After securing the bike, Martin bade me enter the car, opening the passenger door for me like a true gentleman.

'Thank you,' I said.

I glanced at Martin from time to time as he drove. Seeing him in the light of day, I noticed how his newly tanned skin accentuated the beauty of his facial features and his hair was longer than when he had lived in Gran Canaria before, and landed clumsily on his forehead. His eyes were like two burning coals. In the car, silence embraced us, but if one knew how to listen, you could hear the melody of our heartbeats.

I watched out of my window how a flock of seagulls seemed to be following us, dancing and swooping and shrieking.

At last, Martin spoke.

'You are going to kill yourself with this journey, Christina. All that equipment – and riding a bicycle, in this heat? What made you move so far away?'

'For now, it is okay,' I said. 'Gustavo promised to find a different venue for my workshops and art classes, so I would not have to travel so far.'

'Or you could move back closer to the town centre,' he smiled.

'Even though the journey to town takes a while, I love my new house. Once you see it, Martin, you will understand.'

'Tell me about Lima,' I said, hoping to change the subject.

'I will be flying back out there soon,' he said, then looked quickly round at my face and must have seen the sorrow there. 'It will not be a long trip,' he said. with such affection in his eyes. 'Just a few days. I need to make sure that everything runs smoothly there.'

I nodded and looked at his handsome face. I could not believe that he sacrificed himself so much for the welfare of his animals, and I began to wonder if Sofía might have been right about Martin neglecting her daughter for the sake of his work.

'I set up the sanctuary in Lima a few months ago,' Martin said. 'I need to juggle between the two sanctuaries: the one in Gran Canaria and the one over there. We constantly have new arrivals; old, unwanted animals, as I said, destined for the slaughterhouses. Blind, wounded...'

He hesitated and cleared his throat before continuing.

'Also orphans in the wilderness,' he said. 'You must see my sanctuary in Lima one day, Christina.'

He reached for my hand and patted it gently.

I smiled.

'It sounds amazing, Martin,' I said.

But all I could feel was emptiness, knowing he loved something else more than he could ever love me.

I didn't even notice as we pulled up to the house, so lost was I in my thoughts.

'Christina,' Martin said, staring wide-eyed at my little house, 'this place is fabulous. You are so lucky. Come on, you must show me around.'

He laughed and grabbed my hand, looking deep into my eyes. My eyes did not avoid his, as once they might. Instead, they craved the beautiful light I saw there. He squeezed my hand gently.

'I am so happy for you, Christina,' he said, softly.

'Martin,' I said, 'there is something I must tell you. When you were away my ex-husband came. He found me through Marina.'

Martin did not say a word. He simply carried on gazing into my eyes, with so much love.

'He...' my voice broke. Martin reached up and wiped the tears falling from my eyes.

'Go on,' he said, gently, and squeezed my hand. 'It is okay.'

His eyes looked deeper and deeper into mine as if trying to guess what secret they were hiding.

'Martin, I... I am so ashamed.'

'Whatever you have to say, Christina, it really is okay. If you do not want to tell me, that is okay too.' Martin took my hands in his. 'It really is okay.'

I took a deep breath, and closed my eyes.

'Philip, my ex-husband, I... I mean, we... I let him seduce me. I did not feel any love for him, you must understand that, Martin. I felt no love.'

Large tears trickled down my face.

'Hush now, Christina,' Martin said. 'Hush...'

He wiped the hot tears from my eyes with so much tenderness, and I fell sobbing into his arms.

Martin promised to pick me up from my work the following day, but he didn't. No text, no call. He just did not turn up.

I tried to convince myself something had probably come up at work that prevented him leaving, or that he had been called away to Lima on urgent business, but my heart knew none of these to be true.

Days passed. Still nothing from Martin. Dark thoughts swirled around inside me, wreaking havoc in my soul.

CHAPTER FORTY-TWO

The afternoon sun burst from the sky, spilling its hot body onto the beach. A beautiful union of two seagulls played out high above, swooping and soaring together, and I wondered why my life seemed so complicated. I thought of myself and Martin, and the love we had, and wondered how two souls in love could drift so far apart.

I walked into the sea. The waves greeted me bringing relief to my burning feet. As I waded deeper, my body shrank at the cool touch of the water – now up to my shoulders. I plunged my face into the sea and out again, coming up with the taste of salt on my lips and a rushing sound in my ears. My eyes itched. I threw my head back and scraped my hair off my face with my hands.

'Christina! Christina!'

I looked back towards the beach and could see no one. I looked to either side of me at the vast expanse of sea before me – I was utterly alone.

'Christina, Christina! There you are!'

I looked around again – nothing – just the long gleaming beach behind me and the sea stretching itself in front of me.

I took in large lungfuls of air and breathed them slowly out again, trying to quell the blood rushing madly in my veins. The silence around me was deep, and it penetrated my soul.

I sat at the window and gazed at the fading sun while munching on a papaya. The sweetness of the papaya cut through the bitterness in my throat. A week had now passed since I last heard from Martin.

I suddenly felt a strong urge in my heart to go outside. The day was coming to an end slowly there, so I wrapped myself in a light shawl, stretching its light blue fabric over my body and put on my nightgown.

I sat on the steps, and watched the rest of the day go by, the wind whispering softly beautiful stories to me from far away, nourishing my soul.

I wish I could fall in love with the gentle breeze as if it were a person, I thought. In that moment I knew I was in the hands of the godly consciousness. You know me well, I said. You know all of me. You spot the miracles of the simple human being I am. Just tell me why, when my heart is so sweetly in love with Martin, why am I so afraid to commit to a forever dance of souls? I love him with everything I am. He is my life. Sweet wind, please carry these words, these words swelling in my soul, teaching me the meaning of agony. Sweet wind, you know everything. Be the messenger of my heart.

The aroma of wild flowers filled the air, as if in answer.

My feet were getting cold. But it did not matter. I closed my eyes to the gathering darkness and painted the scene in my mind. The pinkish sky like delicate peonies, the slow movement of darkening clouds. How I wished I could stop this night and paint the sky pink again.

Christina, let it be. Let it happen. The laws of nature are irreversible, Christina...

My whole body shivered.

We spend our whole lives trying to change what we cannot control.

My musings were broken by a sudden gust of wind. The coldness of its blows battering my body.

The gentle contour of a golden moon manifested in the sky. I blinked my eyes, slowly got to my feet.

As the cold wind withdrew, it was replaced with a warm breeze.

Isn't it strange, sweet Christina? The wind, how it turns so warm.

I closed my eyes, sinking in the softness of these words, my heart engulfed with love.

Drink it in, my darling baby. Drink it in.

I felt a warm breath on the back of my neck and stood face to face with two glowing eyes, burning with love.

'Let me touch your cheek,' I said, my voice trembling, gently stroking his face with the tips of my fingers. 'Is it you, Martin. Is it really you?'

'It is me, my sweet Christina.'

We fell into each other's arms, our unspoken thoughts and deepest desires sinking in a sacred union of tears. Our faces were scorched hot from each other's touch. We sat down on the threshold of my home. Martin pulled me closer to himself and placed my head on his lap, running his fingers slowly through my hair.

'I am so sorry, Christina,' he whispered.

'What for?'

'I left you thinking I was gone. But my heart told me you were still waiting. I was a fool to let you go.'

He lifted my face to his and showered it with kisses, and my body responded, twisting under the weight of his passion.

'Martin,' I whispered, 'I…'

'… love you,' Martin finished.

We sat on the porch for many hours. The stars blinked at us. Martin stroked my head in his lap and pulled his jacket around me, as the night grew cold.

CHAPTER FORTY-THREE

The morning sun shyly kissed our cheeks.

Martin moved the table and two chairs from my living-room and placed them on the small patch of grass behind the house, and laid some straw about. I picked some flowers and put them in a vase on the table.

I fried some eggs and tomatoes as Martin stood beside me at the stove making a porridge, sweetened pieces of mango and papaya.

Standing there in the kitchen together, preparing our breakfast, a beautiful silence existing between us, it felt as if we had done this a thousand times before.

But there were words I had to say.

'I thought you were never coming back, Martin,' I said.

Martin continued to stir the porridge.

'I needed time, Christina. I threw myself into my work. I...'

'I was lost without you, Martin.'

'I felt it in my heart, my darling. That is why I came back.'

'I am so glad.'

He stared into my eyes.

'There is something you must know about Alejandro,' he said.

'Alejandro?' I said. 'The Seagull Boy?'

'Yes, my darling. Alejandro, the Seagull Boy.'

His face was in his hands as if trying to stop tears from falling, but in vain. A huge flood of tears streamed down his face and a mighty sound came from the bottom of his chest, like the sound of a wounded animal.

I put my hand on his shoulder which shook while he cried.

'What's wrong, darling?' I said.

Gradually his sobbing became quieter till it petered out. He wiped his tears away, his face red from anguish.

'My boy, Alejandro,' he whispered into my ear. My baby...' his voice broke.

I gasped. I couldn't believe what I heard. I drew Martin closer to my body.

'He is an incredible boy, Martin. And you are an incredible father. You two won each other in the lottery,' I whispered tenderly into his ear.

However, my soul was heavy with gloomy thoughts.

So many years Martin had gone unnoticed in the ways that mattered. His own son did not even know who he was.

Martin looked at me sternly, as if he read my mind.

'I cried about not spending time with him for so many years, Christina. I missed his first steps as a baby, his first words. They stole it all from me. His mum, her husband, Sofía. They stole all of it. I hated them for that.'

'You need to forgive them, Martin. I am sure what they did at that time was what they thought best.'

'I can see that now, Christina. But not then. When I left for Lima, I burst into anger and had to throw myself into my work to ease the pain.'

I smiled and kissed his forehead.

'I am so glad, you are back, Martin.'

He kissed me back on my forehead.

'I am back, darling, yes,' he replied. 'For you, and for Alejandro.'

The small breakfast area Martin had constructed offered some shade from the morning sun. I watched his face as he ate. After his return from Lima, he seemed even more handsome – whether it was the deepening of his tan or the relieving of his stress, I could not tell.

After we had cleared the breakfast table, we went back outside, sat on the grass and gazed at the sea, watching the waves dancing happily in the glittering reflection of the sun.

I imagined us always sitting like this together. I smiled. I placed my head on Martin's lap. He stroked my hair tenderly.

'What would you say to dinner tonight on a boat, Christina?'

'Dinner on a boat? That sounds amazing,' I said.

'Dinner on a boat it is then, my darling. Just you and me.'

I swam in the deep blazing fire of his eyes.

'And if you are free tomorrow, Martin, my exhibition opens. I would love for you to be by my side.'

Martin ran his hand through my hair.

'What you have achieved, Christina, is incredible. I am so proud of you. I will do everything to be present, my love.'

He kissed me affectionately on my forehead.

'I know how much your animals mean to you, Martin,' I said. 'But if you could be there around six, it would be so perfect.'

He drew me closer to himself. 'Working with animals is my passion, my darling,' he said, 'but here,' he placed my hand upon his heart, 'here is another passion, a passion for my beautiful Christina – and it will never be extinguished.'

I put my head on Martin's chest, my ear thirstily absorbing the mighty drumming of his heart. I could have stayed there for hours, but then he pulled my face towards him and kissed my lips.

So hungrily did we inhale each other's love, we were soon out of breath. I raised my eyes to the sky and watched the clouds grow dark as if frowning upon our love. But I was not scared of them. I had watched so many people in my life trap me in the shackles of their judgements, I vowed never again to allow any sign of discontent to plant fear in my heart.

The sky grew darker, even menacing. The first droplets of rain fell on our cheeks but could not cool the burning of our love.

Larger droplets of rain plummeted from the sky. Soon we were soaking wet. I unbuttoned Martin's shirt and his chest swelled before my eyes. The rain poured onto it, making it smooth and I ran my fingers through it.

The rain seemed jealous of our love and came down harder. But nothing could stop our urgent caressing as our bodies and souls merged as one.

The exhibition hall was more crowded than I could ever have dreamed. Besides my own work on display, the work of many of the other artists now involved in the project – with the support of myself and Gustavo – filled the walls of the gallery. Everywhere, the excited chatter was punctuated with wild gesticulations and gasps of approval.

One lady, in particular, drew my attention, with her serious features, her brightly coloured outfit and the beautifully oversized feather attached to her hat. The long puffy sleeves of her dress softly embraced her perfect body as she glided across the hall, its laced hem gently touching the floor as she moved. Without realising I was still staring at her, my cheeks blushed as she suddenly stood before me. Our eyes met. She stretched her hand out for me to take.

'You must be Christina,' she said, her stern look transforming into a gorgeous smile.

Transfixed, I examined her features. They were simply stunning. Her nose was of an ideal size, the rosy tint of her cheeks accentuating the beauty of her face. Her eyes were dark and deeply set, and somehow familiar, burning with a passion for life and mystery. Mesmerised by her beauty, I could not speak.

'You are Christina,' she said once more, 'are you not?'

'I am so sorry,' I said, 'I am. Have we met before? I feel like I know you.'

'No, we haven't. I am Isabel.'

We shook hands.

'I have taken a great interest in your work,' she said.

'Oh, I did not realise people talked about me. I am not famous,' I giggled nervously. 'At least, not yet.'

Oh God, what stupidities I was blurting out in the face of this elegant lady. She looked amused and moved a paper fan in front of her face from side to side. The violet roses it was adorned with were of a unique beauty, much like herself, reminding me of my favourite roses from my garden back in England. It was as if this woman was from a different epoch, from a world untainted by modern times.

She brushed her lips with crimson lipstick as if doing so was a statement in itself. Suddenly, Martin burst from out of the crowd and instead of coming straight to me, he approached the mysterious lady and kissed her lovingly on both cheeks.

'Christina,' he said, 'I see you have made the acquaintance of Isabel already?'

A million thoughts raced through my mind. Who is this charming lady? How come he greeted her so affectionately, and how is it he greeted her first and is standing by *her* side instead of mine? Then, as if a wall came tumbling down, revealing what was hidden behind it, I understood.

Martin began to speak, but I did not let him finish.

'I have guests to attend to,' I said, knowing the burning of my cheeks was clearly visible to Martin and his lady friend. I disappeared into the crowd and hurried towards the door.

I was sick and tired of all these situations with Martin.

Why was I so naïve to think Martin would not be affected when I told him of Philip? He is a man, after all, I thought to myself.

All those beautiful memories of myself and Martin dancing in the rain came back to me as I stood alone outside, and all the other special moments we shared. I began to cry and wished a hole would appear in which I could crawl into and disappear forever.

Warm hands snaked around my waist. I pulled away quickly and spun round to face Martin.

'My darling,' Martin said, 'what is the matter? Is everything okay?'

He bent to kiss me. I backed away further. He offered me his trembling hand.

I told Martin I needed to go back to my guests and left him standing outside alone.

The rest of the evening was full of interesting conversations, friendly hugs, and a vivid exchange of artistic views and ideas. It was just what I needed to quiet my thoughts, and to drown out the voice inside me. I giggled a lot. How I loved these affectionate creatures, my fellow artists with whom I shared so much. Gustavo was in top form, and charmed everyone he met, showing me round like a proud father. But through it all, my eyes remained fixed on Martin. He sat at a table with the mysterious Isabel, sending me long, wistful looks which I had great pleasure in ignoring completely.

After Isabel had left, Martin sat alone for a while, then got up and moved around the room, giving the impression to anyone who looked that he was closely examining the work on display, but I knew he was really plucking up the courage to come and speak with me.

Eventually, he did.

'Can we talk, Christina?'

'Why did you do it to me, Martin? Why?'

I wanted to leave him again not waiting for his explanations, but he grabbed my hand.

'I ran like a fool to you, Christina,' he hissed. 'We spent two wonderful days and you think... you think...' his voice broke down.

I shook myself from his grip.

'Here, Martin! Here! Tonight, of all nights! You bring her here! Some– woman who–'

'–is my dear sweet little sister.'

Those eyes of hers. I knew I had seen them before. Those beautiful dark eyes.

'I have not seen her in years, Christina. She lives in the United States. She is in Gran Canaria for a holiday with her husband and her children. She is a painter and a therapist. I brought her here tonight because I knew she would love your work, and to introduce her to the woman that I love.'

His voice was calm and sad.

Even walking barefoot on the streets when I was homeless for a while did not burn my cheeks with the shame I felt in this moment.

'I saw you kissing her with such affection, Martin, and I...'

This time it was my turn to break down, blinded by tears.

And when I wiped them away, he was gone.

How could I have been so stupid?

I faced my paintings as if expecting an answer from them.

But there was none.

I walked back home by myself.

The night was dry, and cooler than the previous night.

I missed the sweet kisses of the rain.

CHAPTER FORTY-FOUR

Next morning I took the first bus and went to Martin's. When I arrived, I felt like it had been my first time walking through the fabulous forest path leading to his beautiful house. The roses dangled idly on the fence as if they watched my face, almost as if we had always shared the same fate – the roses and I – to face the sun, living in constant dread that one day it would be gone. If I didn't find anything positive on my path of life, I would wilt miserably, like them, till I was reborn to bloom again.

I looked around. My hands trembled. Then my whole body shivered, and I uttered Martin's name. My soul ached for him, and pushed me forward. My heartbeat accelerated.

Come on, Christina. You know what you want. Don't hesitate. Knock on the door. Speak to him.

I gathered all the courage I had, and I knocked on the door. I breathed in and out, and I waited, focusing on the subtle sounds around me. I looked around again, needing to ground myself in the sight of nature. I was with my back to the door when I heard heavy footsteps coming up the hallway. I smelled the fresh scent of shaving lotion as the door opened behind me, and I turned round.

'Christina?'

'Please say you forgive me, Martin.'

Silence fell between us. Oh, how I wanted to be in his arms again. The incident at the gallery seemed so stupid to me now. I raised my hand to touch his face. His eyes filled with tears.

'Christina. I am sorry,' he said. 'I should have told you I was bringing my sister with me to the exhibition.'

'Oh, Martin. It is I who should be sorry. To confuse your sister with a secret lover, how can you forgive me?'

'Christina, hush, please. There is nothing to forgive.'

He gently took hold of my hands.

'I want you to meet my sister again,' he said, looking deep into my eyes. 'She is a good person and an amazing artist. She also leads art healing sessions for a circle of women back in the U.S.'

My face beamed.

'I do hope Christina, my love,' Martin continued, 'that we can learn from what happened in the gallery and rise above our fears and enter the space of light.'

It is surprising how many bad memories a human being can hold onto and get prejudiced and scared. I thought my darkness would last forever. I thought I would never be free.

My dear how would you know the light if you hadn't seen the darkness first?

I know, I know.

I was about to speak, but found no words. Martin put a finger to my lips.

'Hush Christina,' he said. 'Let me touch your face. Let me examine that face that once was cut open with so much distrust.'

I laid my forehead upon his shoulder, and wrapped my arms around him.

'Martin, I never told you. I never…'

'What is it?' he murmured.

'You are my sun. The first time I met you I felt the rays of your inner light. I knew that you were special.'

'How come?' he said, pulling back a little to see my face, and laughed free and joyous. 'All you ever did was snap at me!'

'I didn't want it to look like I was interested in a man, just to pull me out of my hopeless situation,' I said.

'You have strength, Christina. This is what I love about you.'

'And you *were* stalking me, Martin. *All* the time!'

We both laughed, and embraced warmly.

'Christina, I can never be seriously angry with you. Even if I feel anger, it does not last.'

Martin's mobile phone rang.

'Excuse me, darling,' he whispered into my ear and answered the phone.

'Martin Stewart speaking... Wounded? Okay. I will be there in twenty minutes.'

He glanced at me.

'Actually,' he continued, 'let me call Dr Moreno. I'll call you back in five minutes.'

Martin immediately called Dr Moreno to arrange the visit. He then relayed the message to whoever had phoned him.

'Dr Moreno will be there in twenty-five minutes,' he said. 'Yes, I'm busy right now. I will see you later.'

Martin put his phone away, and smiled at me.

'I need to go,' I said. 'You might get another call to help with some other wounded animal.'

'No, my darling. Please stay,' he said, and pulled me closer.

'Your animals are waiting. I heard from the phone. You had two badly hurt turtles yesterday,' I said, fiddling with the pocket of my jeans.

He smiled and squeezed my hand. I kissed him on the forehead.

'Dr Moreno is going to the sanctuary,' he said. 'I will be going later in the afternoon. I asked him if we could swap shifts.'

'You did?'

I looked at him in disbelief.

'Yes, my dear Christina. I guessed you might stay for breakfast. I did it for you.'

I smiled, and I kissed his cheek.

'Now come inside,' he said softly, 'it is getting cold out here.'

We sat in the living room, myself and Martin, on the sofa.

'I have decided, Christina,' Martin said, clasping my hands, 'I will not be returning to Lima. My colleagues there are more than capable of tending to the animals. They will manage. I can't be everywhere. Besides,' he continued, 'I need more time for Alejandro and for you, my darling.'

I looked deep into his eyes.

'I love you,' I said.

Martin embraced me. 'I am not going to lose you again, Christina. You are my world, my love. You are everything to me.'

The following morning, Martin went out early and bought an almond cake from Sofía's stall. And as we sat in his kitchen and had a piece of the cake with our coffee, I knew Martin was the one. All I kept thinking over and over was *I love this man, oh, how I love this man*.

Martin dropped me back home when he went to work after lunch. We talked of his sister throughout the journey, and I had made up my mind when I got in to phone her up. I thought that she was an incredible lady. Her occupation impressed me too. Art and healing? Together? I had never thought about it in this way. But yes, art *is* healing, and my art has healed me in my most painful moments.

I sat on my bed, grabbed, Isabel's business card from my bag and dialled her number.

'Hello?'

'Hello. Am I speaking to Isabel?'

'Speaking,' she said, sounding a little strained, then after what sounded like a long breath of relief, she spoke to me in a lighter, almost joyous tone.

'Is that you, Christina?'

'It's me, Isabel,' I said. 'I just wanted to say I am so sorry for the other night.'

'That's okay,' Isabel replied. 'You were busy with your guests. I understand.'

'But you were my guest too, Isabel.'

'Martin explained everything to me, Christina. It's okay. Don't worry.'

'You are too kind, Isabel.'

'How can I be anything other to the woman my brother simply adores?'

I held my breath, and let it out slow.

'Thank you,' I said. 'You have no idea what that means to me, to have you say that.'

'I would really love to meet up with you, Christina, when you have time. Just tell me when you are free.'

'Tomorrow morning?' I said.

'Great. I'm staying at the hotel in the centre of town. Come about eleven, and we could have lunch.'

We agreed to meet about eleven o'clock. I thanked Isabel again, and said goodbye.

'What a sweet family,' I murmured to myself.

I heard a mighty shriek of seagulls and looked out of the window. The sea tossed its body relentlessly, its splashing waves spraying vitriol and anger as the seagulls, like the most skilful surfers, glided above. I marvelled at how the gulls were so serene amidst such chaos, and wished I had their ability to weather a storm so gracefully.

As I entered the hotel lobby, I saw Isabel waiting for me. She wore a turquoise fabric skirt, embroidered with large crimson roses. Her beige shirt hung loosely on her body and her neck was wrapped in a light turquoise shawl. When I approached her, she laid down the book she was reading and stood to greet me. I smelled jasmine perfume on her neck.

After we exchanged greetings, we sat and chatted like old friends. I asked Isabel why she was not staying with Martin.

'He has such a big house,' I said.

'He did offer,' Isabel replied, 'but my husband has business here on this side of the island. Besides, this side of the island has more of an attraction for the artists. I crave meeting them, don't you, Christina? I love that they mostly come from Barcelona or South America too. There are a few Arabs as well. It is interesting how their culture influenced the Spanish one.'

'Ah, the Moors,' I said.

'Indeed,' Isabel said. 'I must introduce you to an Arabic lady I know. You would love her. She passes on the oral poetry and traditional songs of her people to the younger generations.'

'I have never thought about poetry too much,' I said.

'But, Christina, when I look at your paintings, I can *feel* the poetry in it. You *paint* your feelings. Your paintings speak of love, of suffering, of self-discovery and so much more.'

'Both you and Martin are so sensitive, Isabel. Where do you get it from?'

'Our grandma was a nomad. She was raised in a tribe in the forests of Peru. As a child, she used to run barefoot all the time, sing tribal songs and tend to the herds of animals. It was a simple life, but there was so much in it. So much. She inhaled the fresh air coming from the opened door.'

I couldn't believe how similar my story was to the one Isabel was telling me.

'When I was a child,' I said, 'my grandad used to take me to the heart of where the gypsy travellers lived. They led simple life, but how rich.'

'I am leading a group of women, among them all sorts of artists from painters to embroiderers. Would you like to join in our sacred circle?'

'A sacred circle?'

'Yes, we are a group of women that support each other. There are a lot of benefits from that.'

'I would love to,' I said, and felt a big smile spread across my face.

Isabel smiled too. Looking deeply into my eyes, I saw the same light there I saw in Martin's eyes. And like his, they burned fiercely with love and passion.

'Let's go for a walk,' Isabel said.

We marched through the lobby, and out onto the street. The sun dazzled my eyes. The palm trees formed a kind of circle on the adjacent street I hadn't noticed before. A sacred circle, I thought to myself.

The sweet aroma of cinnamon and bananas floated in the air.

We reached the beach and Isabel led me to a small straw hut and a juice stall inside. Colourful bowls of fruit were sat on the counter, and a massive juicer stood in the corner of the stall. A smiling woman put the fruit in the juicer and in seconds a beautiful stream of juice appeared. She poured it into smaller glasses.

Isabel chose mango and I chose my favourite papaya juice. We sat at one of several small tables in the hut, conversing about life and art.

The day was hot, as usual. I imagined the air having sticky hands touching everything around. I felt hot and stifled in my own body. As we talked, I dreamt about a long swim in the cooling waters of the sea.

Isabel's husband came after a while and picked her up. I moved out of the shelter of the hut onto the beach, marvelling at the beauty of the crashing waves.

The seagulls madly circled in the air.

I was already a part of something bigger, I knew that now.

'How was your meeting with my sister?' Martin asked when he came after work to me that evening.

'She is amazing,' I said. 'You and her, you are both so gentle, so sensitive. Oh, I love you, Martin. I love you so much.'

A tear slowly escaped his eye and rolled down his cheek.

'And, my beautiful Christina, I love you too.'

He pressed his cheeks against mine.

I know these burning flames of love will last forever. These hands of his shaping miracles fall softly onto mine each evening. His lips conjure up the sweetest kisses and talk to me using a million wonderful words, and when I need it, they feed me with silence. This soul, the beautiful soul of this man, is my twin flame. His breath calls into existence beautiful things. The invisible becomes tangible within seconds.

Such is the power of love and of dreams.

My little voice sighs with pleasure each day.

Each night our souls mingle into one.

And high above in the deep blue sky, the seagulls play and dance and soar.

EPILOGUE

I yawned and trotted upstairs to the bedroom. I looked at Martin's photo on the night table. Its golden frame shone beautifully. I am not sure which shone more, the frame or the sparkle in Martin's dark eyes.

I already miss him, but I know that I must embark on a new journey with his sister, Isabel. He promised to wait for me. The journey I have planned has no end. No real journey ever does.

Gran Canaria has been my home, my dear beginning of conscious life, but there are more places waiting for me, more places that will awaken the potential lying dormant in my soul.

Martin's heart is one of these places. His love showed me that there is always hope, that there can be happy returns, and that there can be forgiveness.

But I long to see beauty and nature in all parts of this world – this world that God created for me, for Martin, for you and for all human beings.

I have always envied the seagulls, and how they can travel to every corner of this beautiful Earth.

I have always wanted wings.

And now I have them.

About the Author

Living in London, Agnieszka Dryjas-Makhloufi holds an MA in American literature. She teaches ESOL, Health and Social Care at Southwark College. Agnieszka loves spending time in nature observing birds, particularly seagulls. *The journey of seagulls* was born out of her time spent at the seaside in the places across the UK and Mediterranean Sea.

Lightning Source UK Ltd.
Milton Keynes UK
UKHW041222240621
386084UK00001B/53